Falling in Love with Desire

by _L. Elaine_

Acknowledgements

"Don't let the sun go down without saying thank you to someone, and without admitting to yourself that absolutely no one gets this far alone."

~ Stephen King"

There are many to acknowledge! Thank you for all of the encouragement, waiting and hopes that another book would come! Here we are at book five in my *Dynasty of Love* series—this one is another cousin story! While the world has experienced great love, there has been sadness too. It seems like many people who have been foundations in American society have passed on since I released the last book in early 2023. The great poet and author Nikki Giovanni passed away in early December 2024—she inspired my literary journey and desire for English excellence from a little girl; I wonder sometimes if I had been a student of hers what she might have said about my writings in numerous genres. Personal to my family, our Great Aunt Lenear—a matriarch to us, and a fan of my writing, passed away earlier in 2024. She said she was looking forward to this book and hurry up! I know she watches over me and whispers ideas of *Camelot* into my soul along with many of my other ancestors. I dedicate this book to her and will never forget the mantra she held so dear: *family is everything*! To another dear friend, Wilma S. of WULP fame, who passed away in the later part of this year, I say thank you for always loving me, and I will bring your "purple passion" to be the theme of a book one day!

I am grateful to ALL of you even though I could not fit calling everyone by name here: to my friends, family, loved ones, fans now and those who might come to read these books in the *Dynasty of Love* series: Thank you!!! In case you haven't noticed, I love people! Thanks to my Memoir Writing Class family—you all were willing to listen to the early pages and provided invaluable feedback. To Jen Coken, my immense gratitude abounds for that very first book guidance—and the boost that led to my entry into this world of published romance author!! I also thank dear Brenda, who has continued to champion my books at the hair salon. To my Castaway friends—you know who you are—thank you for grounding me daily! To Becca, who lets me ramble about ideas and my crazy, zany and hairbrained thinking—you are the best listener, a Rockstar and I'm working on your heroine story! To Denise M. – you have always been my partner in our insatiable appetite for well-crafted stories of "over the top romance;" let it never stop! To Andra and Ellen, thanks for being mother figures to me now that mom has passed; having you all watch over me and share stories of mom is priceless! To my late father's best friend, Cheese (a nickname that he carried with him for most of his life and so many had no idea that it wasn't his legal name)—may you rest in peace. Just as I was about to publish this book you passed away; thank you for filling in as my father figure for these last eleven years; I get you are forever committed to our family thriving just like dad; and you have kept me connected to dad's legacy which was priceless! I will carry on knowing you and Dad watch over me. To the current and past members of the Warriors A.C., Washington, DC, football team family—it's nothing like having many more brothers watching over me as I walk through life. To my KBC friends and Integrity Group family – you are the wind beneath my wings as we all continue to soar higher; the skies the limit…cheers to infinite possibilities declared in shared word!

Special shout outs to my children and their children; you are the ones I will always claim no matter of birth—my heart beats the happiest tunes because of you! To my blood brother, CC, we are now the living ancestors and I'm grateful for your partnership on this journey! To my son, Alex, thanks for another dynamic cover from my scant details. To Cousin April, thank you for traipsing the world to assist me in researching these adventures; the companionship, the brainstorming, and your feedback of what you like and don't provides an authentic experience in each place; same with Kayla who now has adopted our travel bug! For the reader, know I go these places with you in mind always!! While others are vacationing, I am exploring to bring it back to you in future writings.

Finally, my prayers and well wishes go out to the people in the Andalusian region of Spain. Just before I published this book, there were massive rains that caused floods beyond what could have been predicted or ever wanted. Sadly many lost their lives and homes, towns were destroyed and ways of living forever altered. My desire is that they are able to recover and be stronger than ever! Please let it be…

Introduction

"We travel not to escape life, but for life not to escape us." ~ Anonymous

It's a new year and even as we approach the end of another year, it's definitely time for this book. _Falling in Love with Desire_, the fifth book in the *Dynasty of Love* series—another cousin story from the Gutiérrez clan. I thought I would get this book completed a lot faster, considering the travels I had undertaken to get the essence of those places. However, turns out that the process was not that simple. That saying, "no wine before its time," is the context that I held as I continued the writing process! By the way, you will see the family tree chart missing. Why? The system said the print was too small, so instead of delaying publication, I temporarily deleted it (so stay tuned). People sometimes ask how do I craft these tales. I'll give you my secret: I do a lot of thinking and creative license with the character development; I soak up ideas by walking the paths and streets, staying these places, and sitting in actual restaurants. On my travels, I am sipping on coffee and eating the food, I am watching people and listening. Most would never know there is a romance enthusiast in their mist, anonymously taking notes and photos. I'm also musing! I wonder: what if, what could be a fun conversation to have, what would it be like to ask for what you want, what about the attraction between two people who are unattached—should they pursue it, and what might deliver on the promise of love? I have no answers for you! Just a story I made up!

With this effort, the story of Mira and Xavier, they face daily life and deal with the same basic stuff of human beings! They ask similar questions like the rest of us: should I trust them, should I trust myself, what happens if I am seen in the wrong place at an inopportune moment, what if people get the wrong impression, what do I do with the opinions of my family, what is my culture imposing on me, should I do what's expected or figure out what I want and do that instead?

I plan to take you on many discoveries of places as the heroine, Mira, has the best dream job—travel consultant/arranger to those with wealthy purses willing to discover what's possible, to push the envelope of and pursue life's desires. And Xavier is determined that she discovers his love is a safe place to fall in love and be loved. How did I get this idea? In my youth fresh out of college, a work friend would tell me stories of her sister's travels on the "advance team" for the American government. Before an actual official trip of heads of state, there was a team of envoys who would go in and get things ready for the entourage's arrival. I asked how does one get that job? I thought that was the coolest job one could ever have! Travel to the places everyone wanted to go in the world. Yet, later in life I came to realize a lot of work goes into arranging travels, especially for others who have a certain idea of exactly what they want, but don't know how to tell one how to make it happen. The job was to figure it out, build networks and go experiment. Get it done, as the saying goes! I adopted, "I love to travel" early in life thanks to my grandmother, whom we called Meme; she set aside money so we could go learn about new places, and soak up cultures with childlike wonder! For us, it wasn't a job! And we always asked, where are we going next!

In this book, by far, I could really relate to the heroine's desire to expose people to exotic and unique adventures. So when considering a mate for Xavier, that started my daydreaming about Mira's tale…

Mirasol Katina Morales, an American who hails from and lives in Florida. She is from a well-established family, with parents who are successful lawyers with the proper connections, the right friend circles, and ensured she had a proper upbringing. Along with her parents' love came many expectations for their daughter, an only child. Mira tried the traditional job thing doing something she enjoyed and perhaps originally chose a field to try to please her parents. At some point she decided she wanted to start a business, on her own terms and setting her own schedule, such that she created her own niche company that delivers exotic travel experiences.

Xavier Jose Gutiérrez, is an architect and urban planner by formal education, and is one of the cousins in the infamous family of olive oil conglomerates. He is the son of one of the relatives of Tia Catherine's father Santos Gutiérrez. Xavier has found himself living in New York, far away from his hometown in Spain. He moved to New York a few years prior to the book start to support the family business, Gutiérrez Enterprises. His more important life task was to watch over his father, his only remaining parent, who lived nearby in a senior home. As many seniors who age, they have memories of times gone by and ailments that necessitate different living conditions. Xavier decides it would be good for his father to live by the water again like they did in Spain—both for the memories of his youth as well as the warmer climate. Yet, Spain is not an optimal location as his father doesn't want to be reminded of the painful memories of his wife's untimely death when Xavier and his brother, Matias, were children. Thus, Xavier comes up with a plan to buy some already developed real estate for the winter months so his father could be a snow bird. After asking around, one of his cousins, Valentino, mentions the Florida-based company that arranged his recent honeymoon; and Xavier makes a subsequent phone call soliciting the owner, Mira Morales' assistance. He planned that this job was to be just another consultant he'd hire, even though the task at hand seemed to pose challenges. Upon meeting Mira, Xavier was intrigued by this beautiful, charismatic and no-nonsense woman who creates unique adventures around the globe. He wants her to help him find the perfect home for his father.

Fate had another twist for them, when Mira was unwilling to say yes to him as a client. Xavier discovered a deeper attraction to her he couldn't explain or ignore. In her insistent no on multiple occasions, he remained curious as to why she was unwilling to accept his offer. He'd always previously proven money swayed people if you found the right price. After he finally convinces her to try her hand at being a real estate sherpa for his unique request, he comes up with a way better idea—that they set business aside and go on a date to see what might happen! Mira was a no, no, no to dating as she was absolutely not going to mix business and pleasure. Xavier didn't push…he waited for her to notice she didn't want to resist her attraction for him as well.

Let's go on the roller coaster ride to see if true love blossoms and ultimately wins out. Hopefully, you will discover new places, near and far, seen through the eyes of Mira. Xavier certainly does as he grapples with the walls she continuously erects… Also, on their journey, get a glimpse of two upcoming books intricately connected by the friendships Mira and Xavier continue to cultivate (the stories of Tomas Miguel and Lea, and *Formula One* race car driver, Lella, who finds a love interest while pursuing her dreams to reach the top of a male dominated sport)! Why not have a *Dynasty of Love*…

Prologue

""Life is about making the right decisions and moving on." ~ Walt Whitman

"Hola Dana. I got your voicemail. What do you mean it's over?" Xavier stopped just outside the Johannesburg airport's executive lounge, determined to resolve the issue. This was not how he'd planned to start the first leg of his weekend trip to South Africa.

"Look Xa! We both knew the score. Neither of us were looking for something long term. It was a good time these last few months. And I've changed my mind."

"But Dana, you must know I'm attracted to you. We have mad chemistry together."

"Yes and that's not enough anymore. I've met someone who made me see what I now want. A real relationship. You know, a partner."

"How can you just dismiss me without even seeing if I wanted something more?"

"Do you want something more with me, Xa?"

"I didn't say that? I mean, we are good together. We both work a lot. Your modeling schedule is intense. I like that we got together when it fit our schedule."

"Actually we got together when it fit your schedule, not mine. If you and I were in the same place at the same time. "

"I didn't make any promises."

"I didn't ask you to. I'm convenient to you. No, let me rephrase. I'm was convenient. Not anymore."

"You want more time together?"

"No. I want to be important to someone's life, not just a good time or to be a convenience!"

He shifted the phone. "Look, don't be so hasty. You know I had to go away this weekend and we can talk in person when I get back to New York."

"Yes, you informed me. Why are you away?"

"I told you. My Cousin Valentino, is getting married."

"Exactly! A wedding is a family event to which someone you cared about or who you were in a relationship with, would be invited to accompany you. And it's not like that with us. With you!"

"It's complicated. I can't bring any woman around my Tia Catherine. She'd have interrogated you and had us being the next ones on the marriage block. Thought I'd spare you that."

"Who are you kidding? You are sparing yourself. Goodbye Xa. I hope someday you meet someone who makes you want to risk it all, including standing up to your Aunt."

The line dropped. He had to admit there was nothing Dana had said that wasn't true. Entanglements were complicated. He wanted her to have what she wanted, no matter that it wasn't with him. He wasn't the long-term coupling, companion or partnering type. He much preferred unattached and the ability to be a free spirit. Now all he had to do was survive this wedding and avoid Tia's scrutiny. He turned and walked across the tarmac to board the private jet for his last leg to Cape Town.

Chapter 1

*"You don't have to see the whole staircase, just take
the first step."*
~ Martin Luther King, Jr.

Weeks later…

"Is this Mira Morales?"

"Yes."

"Hello Ms. Morales. You come highly recommended!"

"Oh? Who recommended me?" Mira knew it had to be a high-end client as she only took on new clients through referral.

"My cousin, Valentino Gutiérrez. You planned his honeymoon in Seychelles and Mauritius last month."

"Yes, I did. He was very specific about what he wanted for his bride."

This caller had said the right key words to unlock her services. Name of client, time frame and location. She was always cautious and exclusive. Money for these trips was usually no object and Mira loved that clients in her world let her bring her travel experience, talent and pre-work to create magical adventures around the globe.

"What is your name and how might I help you? Another honeymoon?" She picked up her client doodle pad template to capture some details.

"My name is Xavier Gutiérrez. And no, not a honeymoon. I am not married."

"A couples get away then?"

"No."

"A corporate retreat?"

"No."

Mira was running out of leading questions. Whenever that happened she knew better than to pry too much and to immediately relinquish control to the other person. She said nothing and waited.

"I have to come to the American East Coast. You're based out of Florida, right?"

"Yes, my business is Florida-based." she responded noting he didn't disappoint her theory. She paused again.

"I am thinking to see some beaches where I might look to buy property."

"I am not a real estate agent. Not my forte."

"Yes, I am aware." That was all he said.

"Go on."

"I have always wanted to see the Gulf Coast, Bermuda and Puerto Rico. I will be coming in the first two weeks of December and have to be back home before Christmas."

"Those are quite dramatic seascapes. The weather on the Gulf Coast of America will vary but should be mild; Bermuda in December is often chilly, and Puerto Rico will be in the eighties."

"That doesn't bother me." He was straight to the point, matter of fact.

"Very good. Just a few more questions. How many in your party? What's the style you want? Hotel, resort, house for this visit to meet with me? How do you want to travel? I mean do you have your own plane? Will you require a rental car, or driver?"

"One, you choose, I have a plane, and want to drive myself."

Mira was intrigued by all the variations this stranger presented. It would be a challenge for her and she loved challenges. She was curious why he was traveling alone, and it was none of her business. She was a sucker for a love story for someone else. Maybe he was going to surprise his girlfriend with a later trip or a beachfront house. She provided confidentiality and discretion and never pried into the lives of her customers. The more clients she added to her virtual Rolodex, the more she could fund her own love of travel and adventure.

"Thank you, Mr. Gutiérrez. I only need your contact information and I will e-mail my estimate, plus or minus ten percent for the consultation. I am willing to meet even though I likely will not take the job."

"Cost doesn't matter. Are you able to fly the estimate here to Granada, Spain, so we can meet in person at my office? I only do business with people I meet in person."

His request shocked her. To shock her was rare. "You want me to come to Spain with the estimate?"

"I do indeed. I promise you, like my cousin, I am straight-forward and trustworthy. I just have a business practice of needing to meet with people before I give them my money. You can fly first class, stay wherever you like and we will meet during business hours. I will reimburse one-hundred percent of your costs, plus ten percent fee on your costs for your time. Do we have a deal?"

Wow, wow, wow. She took a quiet deep breath. She liked his style. What he'd presented seemed reasonable.

"Yes, it's a deal. When would you like me there for our meeting?"

"Tomorrow afternoon at four, local time."

Mira would not back down. "See you tomorrow Mr. Gutiérrez."

****

 "Who was that on the phone?" Mira's grandmother Carmen, asked, from across the room.

"A new client. Perhaps." Mira said coming to sit back at the small kitchen table, and sliding her phone back into her bag. Her grandmother, a mere five feet, three inches, with olive skin, and long black hair pinned up in a messy bun atop her head. She was standing at the stove stirring her secret spaghetti sauce. The recipe that tasted divine, made enough for a small army, and had Mira come across town without an invitation.

"I wasn't trying to listen to your conversation. And I think I heard you say you are going to meet a new client tomorrow?"

"Yes. In Spain, actually."

"Spain? Tomorrow? That seems almost impossible!"

"Yes ma'am. It seems like I will be going to Spain. I think I will need to get myself organized and leave for tonight."

"Tonight?"

"Yes, I have to meet with the client tomorrow afternoon in Granada."

"A male or female client?"

Mira hesitated a little too long.

"It's a male! I don't like it!"

"It's all above board. I promise. I am meeting in a corporate office."

"Have you ever been there?"

"I have not. I organized his cousin's honeymoon without actually meeting in person."

"So why are you needing to go all that way to meet this cousin?"

"Oh Grandmummy, don't worry! I will be safe and know how to protect myself. I won't drink or eat anything that is offered. All expenses will be recouped. I'm flying first class, plus my fee." She had used her term of endearment for her grandmother to try to dissuade any concerns.

"It's just a job, Mira. Remember the location might be beautiful and alluring. But you're providing a service. And it's a job, in a strange place. You're not there for vacation."

"Yes ma'am. I know…but maybe a couple hours to tour Granada since I've never been there."

"You don't even know whether you're going to take on this new client." Her grandmother was correct. She only knew this man was a relative of Valentino Gutiérrez.

"Well why did you say yes? Clients come to you. You don't have to go to such trouble. And you don't have to fly to Spain to meet this man."

"I like being challenged. And this is definitely intriguing."

"I don't like it, Mira! You should ask your father what he thinks."

"No, and you will not mention it either. Mums the word! This is business, and I don't need opinions on how to run my business."

"You are so stubborn, just like your father, when you make up your mind. Just be careful. I will wrap up a bowl of spaghetti for you to take with you."

She hopped up and gave her stout grandmother a hug as she stood at the stove. "If you insist! You know, you really are the best Grandmummy ever!"

"Ummmhmmmm. You're just trying to butter me up so you can get extra!"

"If that's what it takes, then call me what you will!"

Mira smiled, her mind already speeding a mile a minute. Game On...Spain...here I come!

Chapter 2

*"Why do you go away? So that you can come back.
So that you can see the place you came from with
new eyes and extra colors. And the people there see
you differently, too. Coming back to where you
started is not the same as never leaving."*
~ Terry Pratchett, A Hat Full of Sky

Xavier stood in his apartment staring out into the city
nightlife. He loved the sense of being on his side of
the window where he controlled the peace. This was
his constant practice of using the window to sort his
thoughts. Fall was coming to Granada, Spain. Being
in the Andalusia region afforded him an opportunity
to check in on his family before he needed to return
back to New York. Scotch in hand in a highball lead
crystal glass, he mindlessly twirled the one ice cube
with his finger. It had just rained making the streets
glisten as passersby rushed to their next
destination. Tomorrow was a full day of meetings
before he went to the family house in Jaen. One
meeting in particular held his interest. The request
that Mira Morales come meet him in person. He
didn't know why he had made such a short-sighted
demand that she come from America to Spain within
twenty-four hours to discuss his business deal. It was
true he typically only did personal business with
people he met face-to-face before executing a
contract. Come to think of it, he could have met her
on United States soil. He wasn't heading back to
New York City until week's end but there was no
urgency to his desire to buy property in Florida.
Maybe he wanted to see if she'd accept the challenge

to show how truly adventurous she was. And she had
without a moment's hesitation.

Xavier would describe himself as a little over the top
in his requests. Most people had a price. One just
needed to find out what it was they desired most, and
determine if they were interested in paying that price.
Travel was no different. It was nice to be home, and
even nicer to be away. Like many, he'd always
wanted to go beyond his neighborhood and
discover. He wondered what Mira Morales price
might be to come halfway around the world. He'd
find out in less than a day's time. He was also
curious, admiring that she had her own niche
business. One that sounded very successful if his
inquiries were correct. Her advice and expertise
would mean he could focus on other endeavors. He
hoped his Papa, Macario, would come spend some
time with him. Spain was not an option, so Florida's
Atlantic Ocean or gulf waters might appeal in lieu of
the cold winter months in New York. In their last
discussion, Papa had said perhaps he'd be willing to
spend some time outside New York. Bermuda and
Puerto Rico were an afterthought he'd given her
because of their close proximity and ease of travel
from New York.

Papa was happily ensconced in an assisted living
home just outside of New York City on Long Island
for most of the year. It was the best money could
buy, and sat right on the water. His being there gave
his brother Matias and himself some peace. Xavier
went to visit once or twice a week or maybe a little

longer between visits when he had to travel outside of New York.

Xavier cherished a work ethic just as they'd been shown as children. He had done his best to stay above the fray, choosing to excel versus get into trouble. In architectural school, he'd taken up urban planning and it had further fueled his desire to see the world. His mantra: leave the last place you visited a little better off than you found it and make obscene amounts of money on the journey! As Julius Caesar had said, *"veni, vidi, vici." "I came, I saw, I conquered."*

For this trip, he'd come home for a long overdue visit with his uncle and aunt, Tio Antonio and Tia Catherine. Without them, he'd be a nobody with not two coins to rub together. They'd watched over him and his sibling after his mother's early death and his father's breakdown. They'd funded his schooling in a trust established for all the children in the family to get a great education. The only condition was to provide the skills one obtained to help family and neighbors. Papa didn't mind whatever Xavier and his brother did for business; and he loved both his sons. Papa's best friend was Tio Antonio—ten years his senior. Everyone always asked about Macario and how well he was doing in America. Only on special occasions did Papa return to Jaen and the family estate. He'd heard him say many times that Spain held too many memories of his younger self.

Xa, as his cousins liked to call him, didn't know much about Tio Antonio's upbringing. According to the stories, he was gone from Granada to its suburb of Jaen when his Papa was very young. And Papa looked up to his cousin Catherine who fell in love with Antonio. His mother and father on the other hand, Xavier knew every detail of their life's stories.

Macario married Maya Alvarez. They were all happy until Mama had gotten killed in a car accident when he was four—the youngest and last child his mother would have. He had very little memory of her. Not like his brother, who was eight. Everyone told him stories about her so he'd not feel lost. As was tradition back then some twenty-eight years ago, a widowed woman with children moved back to her parents' home. Typically the same invitation was not afforded to men. Men were expected to marry again and the new wife would take care of the motherless. Papa had loved Mama with all his heart and was devastated. He felt that he should have died instead of her or at least with his Maya. Papa and Mama went to school together and got married upon graduation, even as Papa's parents thought it a mistake. As the story goes, Macario reached out to his parents for a place to stay so Matias and Xavier would get looked after. Problem was Papa's parents were somewhat stern and none too happy to have little mouths to feed. He still loved their Mama and had no interest in falling in love again, let alone getting remarried. And no woman wanted to raise another woman's love children and live in her shadow, even if her intended was still in his prime. That didn't bother Papa. Even now, on occasion, Xavier would see women fawning over his father in the home. Macario would politely decline their attentions.

When Papa got over his initial breakdown and disbelief about Mama's death, he then got a job, working as a field hand on his family's Gutiérrez land. When he'd earned enough money, he repaid his parents for their short stay and moved his sons into one of the estate's small houses on the hillside olive groves. They had great care, a part-time housekeeper who cooked, and all of them ate supper together every night. Tio and Tia let them run the hills all over the property until they grew into men who were formally educated in school and the family olive oil business. When Papa's parents died, days on the farm were the norm. They along with their cousins were a brood of boys, over a dozen in total between all the generations. Those were the best of times! Xavier still remembered how Tia would bake cookies for them after school. They were warm when she opened the front door in greeting, plate in hand overflowing with treats. If you were well behaved in school, you got an extra cookie. If not, you got none. That was a great reward-penalty structure to teach. They were also taught, *Family is Everything*! His cousins, like brothers to him, always brought lots of antics, teasing and pranks whenever they were together. Everyone looked out for each other as was expected in a big family. Even though now they were all grown up, they had remained in close communication, with the age differences creating natural alliances amongst them. Xavier didn't easily trust people outside his massive Gutiérrez clan. He'd really had no need to. Appearances mattered, and they were told not to tell their secrets to those external to the family—be wary of people who might exploit you for their own selfish desires. Having a famous family, a well-known name and money had made them a target of fake friends, opportunists, and leaches. They were also told not to flaunt their wealth, no matter how hard earned; and to be generous with the less fortunate. Xavier had seen some of his cousins be the recipient of unwanted attention, be invited to out-of-control parties and debauchery. He'd been sent out to the cousins in need of rescue on many occasions. All of that was fodder for the tabloids who could not get enough always publicizing sensational details, regardless of the truth.

Xavier appreciated remaining occupied with worthy endeavors. He worked. When he completed school, he'd learned the business from the ground up. That was where his reliance on family shaped his habits. He designed all the new offices for the family in this modern era, and had also been asked to oversee the New York operations. Over time, business dealings grew into networks, and those linkages bore successes that built partnerships. A handshake and face-to-face interactions were hard to fake. One could tell a lot about someone from in-person meetings. Many schoolmates had hatched get rich quick schemes, or pitched ideas for using his money for some startup company. Xavier preferred to lend his support to his family.

As the door to his home office opened, he swallowed the remaining scotch, blocking out the past.

"Senor, I made a plate for you. If you don't need anything else, I will leave for the evening."

Tia Catherine had sent over her chef to cook him dinner after he'd said he had too much work to return back to Jaen tonight. 'You must eat!' he remembered his aunt's exclamation. There was no refusing Tia. He'd let Ms. Santori in a couple hours ago at half past eight. Traditional dinner in Spain was around eleven; even though Tio and Tia now preferred eating about seven.

"Thank you, Ms. Santori. I think I can make due. Please tell Tia thank you as well."

"Of course Senor. I cleaned the dishes, and put the leftovers into containers that you can eat or freeze."

"Great idea! Have a good night." He had no doubt the older woman was following exact directions.

There was no point in contradicting Tia Catherine. He hadn't even mentioned he was in town. Perhaps he thought he would surprise Tia and Tio. She had radar, or extra sensory perception. And she used it for their best interests. At least most of the time. There were a few exceptions. Like her uncanny knack for playing matchmaker. He had no interest in such foolish endeavors. Settling down was best left to his cousins. Which reminded him, he needed to check in on his other cousins. Tomas Miguel, TM they called him for short, was his best friend, and definitely a handful by himself. Likely being the youngest of six brothers left one wanting for more attention. All of them had been loved equally. TM was spoiled, and used to getting his way. Xavier had done his best to keep him from ending up in the daily news. Sometimes it worked and other times, they both ended up in the tabloids. He didn't mind most of the time because there was lots of laughter on the other end of a night out. The Gutiérrez name brought with it fame and notoriety, without any of them needing to be listed by name. On more than one occasion, Tio and Tia had sent him to fetch his cousin out of some trouble because TM had failed to mention his plans. While sorting out his Papa's happiness was important, Xavier was also equally concerned about TM, and determined to keep him from spiraling out of control living the playboy lifestyle. Life was a process of steps to take. If only he could tie his cousin up and lock him in a tower until he came to his senses. Hell, TM might die an old man before that ever happened.

The patter of rain had him turn back to the window. In the midst of the downpour, he sighed to himself. Tomorrow would sort itself out. He'd be able to tell from his meeting with Ms. Morales if she was the right person for the job or not. For now though, he was calling it a night.

Chapter 3

"To move, to breathe, to fly, to float, to gain all while you give, to roam the roads of lands remote, to travel is to live." ~ Hans Christian Anderson

The next day…

"Hey Scoot!"

"Hi Dad." She responded knowing he loved to call her by his pet name, reminiscent of her baby days.

"Where are you? I called a few times."

"I just landed in Spain. I'm working."

"Spain? That's halfway around the world!"

"Yes, well that's the nature of my job Dad. Lots of traveling."

"Your mom and I worry about you. It's not safe for a single woman to traipse around alone."

"Dad that's old fashioned. I'm careful. My assistant knows where I am at all times. If I need security, I hire it."

"That doesn't mean we don't worry. You should settle down, get a regular job."

"No! That's not my dream."

"Just think about it, okay?" She was in no mood for a lecture.

"Was there something you needed Dad. I'm about to step into a client meeting?"

"Your mom and I want you to come home for Thanksgiving. Your grandmother has said yes. Mom thought I should call to get it on your calendar."

"I'll see if my calendar is open. I won't make any promises beyond that."

"If you had a regular job, then you'd be off and free to come home."

"Bye Dad! Sending my love to you and mom." Before he could say another word, she clicked off. She loved her parents, and yet the thought of going home for the holidays was as appealing as a root canal. They would spend the time comparing her to other normal people. You know, people with good children who work regular jobs, and are married with children. No thank you! At twenty-seven years old, she had no interest in doing anything other than having her business elevate up to the next level, and so on.

Mira stepped through the doorway of Gutiérrez Enterprises building on the Calle Reyes Católicos, which the hotel explained is the main shopping street. An impressive, five-story, corner building, in opaque gold color and architecture from time long ago gone. The double-glass doors, framed in brown wood were heavy and imposing. Inside the lobby, the epitome of luxury in its inner sanctum. Chairs of cherry wood and matching peach cushions were littered discretely around the long hallway. There also, three domed archways, with black, white and gold accents that perfectly matched the high gloss, marble floors of similar colors. On the left wall, a giant, circular mirror with black and gold accents. The opposite wall held an understated painting of the Spanish countryside and olive groves. On both sides of the archways, side tables with large floral arrangements. At the end of the hallway was the last domed archway above another set of double wooden doors. There was no reception desk. Mira watched the doors open and a petite woman with black hair in an above shoulder length, olive skin tones, rimmed glasses and a welcoming smile walked towards her. She was dressed in a simple black skirt, and matching jacket. The sheath of a shirt that could be seen was a pale gold. Her whole look matched the scene, and Mira felt like she didn't get the memo. Why? In contrast, she was dressed in navy fitted trousers, and a baby blue blouse she'd changed into at the hotel. Flying overnight, left her somewhat tired, even though she was excited to be in such a beautiful city. And now, loving the elegance of her surroundings.

"Ms. Morales, my name is Ana." The woman offered her dainty hand to Mira.

Mira returned the gesture. "Nice to meet you Ana. Please call me Mira."

"Please follow me and I will take you to Mr. Gutiérrez's office."

"That would be lovely."

Mira followed the woman back to where she'd originally emerged. Just inside the brown-framed arched doorway, Ana stopped at what looked to be an elevator. Gold doors, that opened to a wood paneled compartment. They walked in. She and Ana stood silently as the doors closed. When the doors reopened on floor five, they were greeted by another long hallway that matched the décor of the first floor. Mira was impressed, recognizing that whoever designed these offices had exquisite taste. There were no names or numbers on the imposing brown wooden doors as they walked by. At the end of the hallway, Ana stopped and turned the doorknob. It gave way and she walked through to another reception area, with Mira following closely behind. This inner sanctuary held a traditional reception area. Across from the door, a mahogany desk, which Mira assumed belonged to beautiful, bubbly Ana herself. Straight ahead about ten feet, another closed door. Ana approached it, then knocked on it, and immediately turned the knob not waiting for someone to open it.

****

"Senor, may I present Ms. Mirasol Morales." Mira heard as she walked into the office.

Xavier turned from the window where he'd been peacefully observing the chaos on Granada's busiest shopping street.

"Thank you, Ana. Ms. Morales, nice to meet you." He watched as Mirasol Morales stepped around Ana to come forward, stopping in the middle of the room to offer her hand.

"Senor Gutiérrez, thank you for having me." Cat-like, piercing brown eyes met his gaze, drilling through his coolness into his soul. He felt an immediate flame as she pulled the breath from his lungs faster than a breeze blew out a flame. He cleared his throat.

"Please have a seat," he offered one of the two high-back leather chairs that sat in front of his desk. He paused, trying to decide if he would sit next to her or put his desk between them. Deciding on the later, he turned to move around the large wooden structure that had been in his family for generations.

"Thank you for coming to Spain for our meeting." Xavier said as he sat down casually.

"Not a problem at all. However, as I said over the phone, I do not believe I am the right consultant for you."

He steepled his fingers together as he leaned back in his matching leather executive seat. It had been customized for him, such that it created an imposing air of authority that their business commanded on his home turf. He didn't particularly appreciate the need to exact his authority over anyone. If at all possible, he preferred compromise and partnership.

'I think you are the perfect consultant for me." Xavier hadn't thought much about anyone declining his offer. He knew if she'd come all this way, that she was either interested or at least he had a shot of getting her to acquiesce with the right amount of monetary incentive.

"Why?"

"That is a very interesting question, Ms. Morales. People don't often ask me why."

"I don't mean to offend you, Senor Gutiérrez."

"None taken. And please call me Xavier or Xa. If we are going to work together, calling me by my father's name will never do."

"I didn't exactly say yes to working with you. Please don't mistake my taking this meeting as evidence that I agree."

He smiled. She was breathtakingly beautiful, and determined that he not presume he had won. How could he feign offence? She was spunky, and strictly business. He'd seen his portion of beautiful women, dated his fair share too. And even still, he'd seen none like her with her smooth olive skin, petite frame, ample bosom, and curvy hips. She was made for lovemaking. He'd never stopped to consider his high-end destinations' agent would be drop dead gorgeous. Not that it would pose a problem. Business was business, and he always kept it platonic and separate from his desire for pleasure.

"You're correct Ms. Morales. How about you go through your normal process, and keep an open mind to determine if you are willing to help me in a way I know you are capable of?"

She didn't smile back at him. He watched her tilt her head as she considered his request. She seemed wary. Was he using a different tactic? Absolutely, and he couldn't wait to see what her answer would be.

"Okay. That seems fair since you brought me all this way, and are reimbursing all my expenses, plus my fee."

"Very good. Would you prefer coffee or tea? I will ask Ana to bring in service."

"Tea would be lovely." Even though she'd promised her grandmother she wouldn't eat or drink anything, that was only to alleviate worry. Mira had no worries that this meeting would be anything other than a business meeting and she would not insult her host by declining a customary tea.

Chapter 4

"Every step is on the path." ~ Laozi

Once the beverage service had been provided, Mira put her teacup back on the saucer and set it upon the circular conference table. Xavier sat just to her right with his coffee, which he drank black. Mira pulled her tablet from her bag that sat on the floor.

"Typically I start with a casual conversation, peppered with some questions."

"That sounds reasonable. I'm ready to answer any questions."

"Why hire my firm?"

"You come highly recommended. I trust my cousins, and they were very impressed. Your reviews are stellar, yet your public advertising is non-existent. That leads me to believe you have a work ethic that is to be appreciated."

"Thank you! My clients are always satisfied because we go above and beyond to hear their desires. I listen, and I am honest. I do not advertise. I only take on new clients through referrals, nor will I just take on anyone, no matter how much money they offer."

"That is important to me. I get your hidden message as well. Ms. Morales, I am not trying to throw money at you to get my way."

"Why do you want me to arrange this tour of Florida?"

"I will be candid. My Papa is getting older and the cold is not good for his ailing body. So I promised him a winter warm location. Hence the idea of Florida in the United States. He wants to be a snow bird, as I believe you Americans call the escape from the North. Also, he says he desires to be closer to me for part of the year."

"And what does your mother say?"

"Mama died years ago when my brother and I were young."

"I'm sorry."

"Don't be. I've had a long time to adjust."

"Oh?"

"I love my Papa. Surely you can understand my need to make my last living parent happy."

"I do indeed. My parents are getting on in years and always complaining about my need to come visit them."

"You don't live at home?"

"Gosh no! I don't even live in the same town as them. I moved away after school. I am not too far away though."

"But you are a single woman, no?"

"What does that mean?"

He paused. "I meant no offense. In Spain, we tend to live at home until we marry and if women move away, they don't live alone."

"Things are different in America."

"Yes I'm aware."

"Anyway, back to the business at hand."

"You have quite a repertoire of adventures, Valentino says. Travels to over one hundred countries for a worldwide client list."

"Yes, well I cater to adventurous personalities, I believe. Anyone can go on a vacation or a trip. I deliver experiences."

"That is why I invited you here."

"Yes, so you've said. I am not a real estate agent though."

"I want to hear of your experiences in Florida so I can determine the best place to land. Papa is a bit stubborn and fussy. He says it is his right as an 'aging man.'" Xavier did air quotes for emphasis.

"I have had quite a few experienced travels of
age. Once, a woman turning one hundred years old
wanted to learn how to surf on Waikiki Beach,
Hawaii for her birthday. That included an immersion
surfer slang class, lots of early mornings, and tropical
non-alcoholic drinks, as she gave up drinking in her
seventies. It was a blast!"

"Papa is in his seventies and he doesn't seem the least
bit interested in giving up his daily Sangria. He
makes a fresh batch daily."

"Well I guess all senior folks are not the same."

"Definitely creative." She could tell he was trying to
keep a straight face.

"I just hoped she didn't die on my watch. Turned out,
as a centenarian, she possessed way more energy than
me."

"You surfed?"

"Not on that trip. I usually set things up and then
once the trip begins I move on. However, the client
was adamant that her family not be there. So they
made me promise to stay close, just in case."

"Did it all work out?"

"Of course. It was my job to make sure it did."

"What is Waikiki like? I've heard stories of the
turquoise waters. *Blue Hawaii* people talk about."

"It is beautiful, busy and full of surfers. People are always walking the beach with surf boards. In the backdrop is *Diamond Head Mountain*."

"People live on the beach?"

"Yes, in some areas. That area has multiple subsections; some hotels and condos on the beach and some being across the street. People sit out, sunbathe and swim. It is the mecca of surfing or even to say "*I surfed Waikiki Beach*." Just before sunrise, surfers flock to the water so they are in the waves as the sun lightens it; then maybe they come back for sunset, which is breathtakingly magical from that beach. Surfing until dark because the waves are always best at those times."

"I can't imagine such a life where one organizes their day around surfing instead of working. I have worked in the family business since my formal schooling ended. Even though I travel, there is a definite separation of business and pleasure."

"I understand. Waikiki is a must see at least once in everyone's lifetime. Like most places, there are tourist industries, restaurants for tourists and locals, businesses, government offices and every kind of service to support human beings who live on islands. Those who grow up at the beach often take for granted that people travel near and far to experience what they have always possessed and possibly ignore."

"Thank you, Ms. Morales, for giving me a glimpse of your view into that world you have so masterfully illustrated."

"Of course. And please call me Mira." She didn't like Mirasol, and she could be friendly.

"Do you like adventure Mira?" He hadn't skipped a beat. The way he said her name in his thick native accent, sounded to her like caramel lovingly being drizzled over the top of ice cream.

"I think so."

"What's the most adventurous thing you've ever done?"

Her first thought was coming here to Spain. And she didn't want to give him the wrong impression.

"Have there been so many you can't choose?" His words invaded her thoughts.

"Yes and no."

"Lo no entiendo."

She knew Spanish. He was saying he didn't understand her answer.

She would not be phased. Was he testing her resume? She hoped not. She answered in English as if she didn't need to explain. "Yes, I have been on many adventures, as you say. And in comparison, to all possible adventures, many is subjective. They are all different."

"Ah I see. What was the one you would like most to do again?"

"Anything spa related."

"Not what I expected as an answer!"

"Mr. Gutiérrez, I work quite a bit. It is not just myself I have to be responsible for. The opportunity to relax is priceless to me."

"Remember we agreed to being on first name basis? I am not judging you. It is a fascinating answer that surprised me."

"Right. Xavier."

"That's better. I am not sure I ever relax. I work. I have times when I am not working. Relax? Probably never."

"You should try it sometime."

"Perhaps."

"Next, I have an online questionnaire for you to fill out." She handed him the card with the scan code or url that was linked to her database.

"How long will that take?"

"Fifteen minutes or so depending on how decisive you are about your needs. However, remember it is geared towards travel adventures, not buying property."

"Understood. Not a problem. What will you do while I complete the questionnaire?"

"Stare out the window."

"I could have Ana give you a tour of our offices. I designed the renovations of the building."

"With all due respect, I decline. I really can entertain myself."

"Suit yourself." Mira watched as Mr. Gutiérrez, Xavier, got up and walked to his desk. There he hit a hidden button, and the desk opened to produce a screen. She assumed it was the latest technology that a businessman would have to organize his need for a computer. She had little interest in traditional office work. She made a few notes on her tablet, and then turned her attention to the window.

Mira's phone buzzed at the exact moment he pressed the submit button. She had synced her business program to alert her to new data and communications, especially when she was on travel. She had a monitored twenty-four hours a day service for emergencies where one could get a human person to communicate. She was typically the one to pick up if she had signal, wasn't in a meeting or on an airplane. For the amount of money her clients spent, they expected her to cater to them without question.

"I'm done." While Mira knew she was the only one in the office space with him, he still startled her in breaking the silence.

"Thank you for completing my intake questionnaire." She turned slightly in her chair to look over her shoulder. He was returning back to the conference table.

He handed her back the card. "It was quite thorough. While a lot of it didn't apply because of the nature of my request, I appreciate your asking a similar question from multiple angles."

"I find that it gives me a sense of what matters to those seeking my services."

"Si. I imagine it also brings to the forefront when people think they're being decisive and in reality, they're actually being wishy-washy."

"I suppose it does. I just appreciate actually hearing their desires so I can look for said and unsaid messages. It definitely gives me a leg up to cater to them if at all possible."

"What's next?"

"I have to go back and consider your responses to see if there's a good fit. And I have a flight to catch."

"You're not staying in Granada for a few days?"

"Absolutely not. I have to get back to Florida by tomorrow. I have another meeting in two days."

"How will we communicate after your consideration?"

"I will call you?"

"What if I come to Florida earlier than my plan?" Xavier hadn't meant to suggest he would rearrange his schedule. And he liked the idea of seeing her again, sooner rather than later.

"I thought you said December in our conversation, yesterday."

"I did. And I have the ability to change my mind."

"Suit yourself. I will have my assistant reach out to get a meeting on the calendar that fits into both our schedules."

"Excellent. It has been a pleasure Mira. I am convinced that working together will be lucrative and fulfilling all around."

"We shall see, Xavier," she said arising from the chair.

"I will walk you out."

"No, I am sure I can find my way." She dropped her pad in her bag, and put the strap on her shoulder.

"I insist. Also, please send your bill to me, as we agreed."

Mira said, "I will get it to you by tomorrow." She followed him to the door, that he handily opened for her.

"Senor, I will see Ms. Morales out."

"No, no, I will do the honor."

Mira bit her lip and followed to the elevator bank. He easily pressed the button, and the doors parted as if they knew he was there. She was silent watching the numbers decrease until they arrived at floor zero—the lobby level annotated as such in most European cities. When the doors reopened, he let her proceed ahead of him. She walked confidently across the lobby of opulence. Just inside the glass outer doors she stopped, and turned towards him.

"Thank you again for making time into your schedule to share your desires." She stretched her hand out to shake his.

"The pleasure has been all mine Mira. See in you Florida." They shook, and for the first time in a very long time Mira got the feeling that she couldn't wait to see him again—a rare desire indeed, and one she never felt for clients.

She turned back toward the street and walked out the open door into the afternoon sun. Once on the sidewalk, she hurried around the corner. That meeting had not been what she'd expected. Yes, her new wanna-be client was gorgeous with his jet-black, curly hair, olive skin and muscular body. Even if it might be smashed into his fitted black suit, with matching shirt and tie, Mira could tell it hid very little of his healthy physique. He had brooding, amber brown eyes, and a cool demeanor. Just below the surface she sensed a controlled sizzle that fueled her caution. Not because she was afraid of him. Instead she was afraid of her desire to move just a little closer to him. He had on the sexiest cologne of lemon with a hint of vanilla. And she would just bet he could go from cool apathy to red-hot passion in seconds. It was attractive as hell! She understood why her preliminary research of this man as a possible client came with grainy photographs from paparazzi who stalk the rich and famous—he is one of "the beautiful people" in the world.

Mira shook her head to try to clear her mind. Her assessment of Xavier was not comforting. It might just be in Mira's best interest to say no to this job. She would have to steel herself against his allure, his charm, her desire. Especially before their next encounter she'd already agreed to host back in Florida.

Chapter 5

"The foundation of family—that's where it all begins for me." ~ Faith Hill

Two Days Later

Mira walked out of her inner office, and before her stood "the Xavier Gutiérrez" in her small, reception area. His imposing six foot, plus frame didn't fit into her space. Perhaps she didn't want him to fit into her world.

"Mira, it is good to see you again. I really appreciate you fitting me into your schedule." He offered his hand, and of course she placed her hand into his.

"I happened to have some time this morning. Thank Miguel, as he is a miracle worker with my calendar."

"Gracias, Miguel."

"El placer es mío."

Mira ignored the exchange in Spanish between her assistant and Xavier.

"Please come into my office. I don't have as opulent accommodation as your beautiful Granada offices."

"This is a very welcoming space," he said as he moved past her and she caught a whiff of his subtle intoxicating scent. Today he was dressed in a royal blue suit, open colored white shirt, and hair slicked back. Mira hesitated to close her office door. She felt like she needed a chaperone with this man. *Nonsense Mira—this is your turf.* A quick breath later, and she pushed the door closed.

"Were you able to come up with an initial game plan for my search?"

Mira walked to her desk, as she watched Xavier select the chair on the right. *Focus yourself Mira,* she chided her mind. *He is a client. Well he might be a client.*

"Not fully. I'm still sorting through a list of possible Florida cities with residences based on your survey responses."

"That sounds promising."

"Let's not get ahead of ourselves."

"What did you glean from my answers?"

"It was clear that you are looking for places that are on the beach or near the beach."

"Correct. Papa likes the beach, and being able to take a walk when the mood suits him. Not so much that it is mandatory to be on the beach, and definitely with a sea breeze."

"Yes, well there are many choices in Florida."

"I did note that I am interested in Bermuda and Puerto Rico."

"I couldn't tell whether you had a preference."

"I hear they are both beautiful places."

"No, I mean whether you want to live in Florida, Bermuda or Puerto Rico."

"The jury's still out. Probably Papa will prefer mainland. I haven't quite convinced him to totally abandon New York."

"Bermuda to New York is an easy nonstop flight, a little over two hours."

"That is good information to have. What about to Puerto Rico?"

"Likely about four hours. Will you fly private jet or commercial?"

"Papa hates private jets. He thinks it's a waste of money and fuel."

Mira made notes in her computer as Xavier talked. She wanted to get a feel for his preferences and choices.

"Where would you go?"

"Go?" She looked up from the computer screen into amber eyes staring at her. She continued to type, even while giving him a questioning stare.

"You know, if you were filling out your own questionnaire."

"Oh! I can go anywhere. The luxury of a world at one's fingertips."

"Let me rephrase. Where would you like to explore if not working?'

She paused, leaning back in her chair. "Give me a minute to think." No one had asked her that question in years. Rarely did she stop to consider travel if it wasn't for work, nor did she entertain her own wants or desires. An occupational hazard she supposed. Sorting through the catalog of continents, there was always a place to go.

"Munich maybe." That was the last commercial she could remember seeing on some travel channel and wondering what might it be like to visit.

"I have a residence there."

"Really? Tell me, what's it like? Bavaria looks beautiful. Everyone talks about *Oktoberfest*. Yet, from photos and marketing materials, it seems charming without one having to consume beer at a festival this time of year."

"It is a wonderful place. Charming indeed. Lots of walking squares, beautiful architecture, markets, clean air and genuine people."

"Perhaps one day I will get there."

"None of your clients have asked for a trip there?"

"No. I suppose it's easy to organize going there for the typical things to do."

"Maybe, once I've gotten Papa settled, I'll hire you to go there."

"Hmph, that's an amusing idea. Hiring me to go to a place you've been to and have a residence."

"I'd love for you to have reason to see it."

"Then it won't be personal exploration, will it?"

"I suppose not. Give me a bit of time to expand on it. I'll shelve the idea temporarily."

She laughed. "Okay."

"Tell me some of your adventures?"

Again, Mira was caught off guard. He'd asked another rarely asked question. Most often people were interested in their plans, not in the adventures Mira had organized. On occasion, people might ask for ideas, and then when they saw her travel portfolio albums, they would focus in on one or two destinations.

"Let's see: Honeymoons in Seychelles and Mauritius- a nod to your cousin; Bermuda for sailing and sun bathing on pink sands, St Croix snorkeling at Cane Bay, St. John's for camping in St. John's Bay, studying flora and fauna at El Yunque National Rainforest in Puerto Rico, oh yeah, there was also kayaking in a Bioluminescent Bay near Vieques. Marathon Shopping in Dubai, dinners in Paris, safaris in Africa, painting the classics in Rome, donkey trip down the Grand Canyon in Arizona, movie premieres in Hollywood, hiking the Appalachian Trail, glamping at the Sturgis Motorcycle Rally in South Dakota, Mt. Rushmore hikes there too. Then there's endless girl's trips: Las Vegas, Nevada, South Beach in Florida or SoBe—that's what they call it…very popular for bachelorette parties. For typical women, anywhere there's a spa, hot springs, mud baths. Paris Fashion Weeks is also a recent, high-end event for those who want to be connected. Extreme sports such as diving the *Blue Hole* in Belize and Australia's *Great Barrier Reef*, Surfing Waikiki in Hawaii; then there's the archaeological digs in Egypt, historic talks of the Battleships in Pearl Harbor. I could go on…

"Wow! You've been busy."

"Yes, enough so I have a staff of four to assist me with keeping much of it sorted."

"Where are the best beaches?"

"All over."

"Unique ones, then?"

"Antigua boasts three-hundred and sixty-five beaches—one for every day of the year. Punta Cana in Dominican Republic has soft white sands, and huge mega-mansions that can be rented. But then so does Grand Cayman have beautiful white sands. Hawaii's Maui has turquoise clear waters; yet so does Cozumel off the east coast of Mexico's Yucatan Peninsula. Thailand has Phuket and Ko Phi Phi. It's breathtaking in Seychelles and Mauritius too…likely because they're in the Indian Ocean. I've not yet discovered Turks and Caicos, Fiji, Bora Bora, Tahiti or Goa—I hear they are equally unique. Oh, the Maldives is upcoming for couples get away, and Costa Rica for beach and jungle theme. There's somewhere for theme of beach and paint that I can't remember right now.

"Which beaches have the prettiest water?"

"According to me?"

"Of course!"

"I guess it depends on the color of the water you like. I like varying colors as the day goes by. Some of the most beautiful water I've seen was in Destin, Florida. Oh, and St. Croix in the U.S. Virgin Islands as well as St. John have beautiful colors. You mentioned Bermuda…along the coast in St. George Town. It is one of the most beautiful and close to the East Coast."

"What's been the most extreme thing you had to do?"

"Kite surfing off the coast in Mauritius."

"Tell me about it?"

"Perhaps another time. It's not a short story and we're almost out of time. I like to stay on schedule."

"I can appreciate that. Where's next?"

"I have to go to Aruba on a business trip later this week."

"You don't let any grass grow under your feet."

"I don't have that luxury."

"Where are you staying? I have a residence there."

"Do you have a residence everywhere?"

"I don't. However, my family's interests require I travel quite a lot. If I have to go multiple times to those places, then I look into a residence so I can have my own conveniences."

"I can understand that. In Aruba, I'm staying at the *Ritz Carlton*. By far my favorite establishment so far on island. We'll see what the *St. Regis* has to offer when it's finished. Where is your residence?"

"*The Ritz* as well. A fine establishment. Do you mind if I tag along to watch you work?"

She paused. "I haven't said yes to taking you on as a client."

"I'm confident you will though. How about I meet you in Aruba and we can discuss further?"

Mira clicked back on her keyboard, bringing the computer out of sleep mode. Then she pulled up her calendar to confirm her schedule, the day after tomorrow. Miguel was very reliable to keep all her appointments.

"Okay, I will meet you for breakfast at the hotel restaurant. Let's say at nine, Friday?"

"Deal!" He quickly agreed.

She hopped up from her high back chair, and walked around her desk. She reached out her hand. Sealing the deal with a handshake was good business. He shook her hand and she could feel nothing but warmth coupled with controlled strength emanating from his grip.

"Deal. Now if you'll excuse me Mr. Gutiérrez, I have more calls to make."

"Remember, call me Xavier, or Xa, as those who know me do." He smiled, shaking his head up and down, as if confirming she was someone who could be on a first name basis.

"I will remember next time, Xavier. I'll see you Friday."

"Si, you will. See you in paradise, Mira."

She watched as he walked away from her after purring her name in his native Spanish accent.

When the door closed, she returned to her desk chair spinning to look out the window. She wasn't sure why she remained intrigued by this man. Already she missed listening to his voice, and watching his expressions of challenge as she sorted through her wariness with having him as a client. She thought him being on her turf would sway the playing field. It hadn't. He'd swept in commanding attention from her and her trusted assistant. Miguel had swooned, which was unlike him to capitulate to a client. He'd buzzed her immediately already knowing she was on a client call right up to her appointment with Xavier. Their meeting was to start at ten-thirty in the morning and he'd arrived a whole thirty minutes early. It threw her office into upheaval; it threw her into discomfort. Clearly Xavier Gutiérrez, had unlimited resources. He could hire an army of real estate agents, better versed in all Florida has to offer. Why her? She didn't have the slightest idea.

And how in the world had he insinuated himself to show up in Aruba? She didn't mind potential clients investigating her work—an area in which she had unbounded passion and energy to leave highly satisfied customers. Typically though they remained local or watched her marketing videos for different locales. He'd surprised her, even suggesting he would fly all the way to Aruba. *"I have a residence there."* She wondered about all these residences. Perhaps a mistress in every city—the playboy life. No matter, Mira had to be in Aruba, and she wouldn't have to babysit him or make any arrangements. He would find his own way and he had his own place. *No big deal, Mira...*or at least she hoped she didn't regret saying yes.

Four days, later...

"There you are?"

Mira looked up from her notepad. Xavier had found her. She'd literally just arrived about four minutes prior—purposefully interested in seeing if he would already be there. When he wasn't, she'd smiled to herself. He would arrive momentarily she knew because he'd been early the day before yesterday. It was like cat and mouse.

"Good Morning Xavier."

She was about to get up.

"Don't get up on my account. May I join you?"

"Of course. I just arrived."

"How is your day so far."

"Lovely. The sun is up in paradise."

"Indeed."

The waitress made a beeline for their table.

"Good morning Sir. Are you having coffee, juice or both?"

Mira suppressed her knowing smile. She knew women. They wanted to get closer to him, get his attention, shoot their shot. Being that Xavier had a residence here, he was likely on the radar of such a resort with stellar service.

"Black coffee please."

"Yes Sir. I will be right back."

The woman was back in five steps with hot coffee being poured into the cup already placed on the table.

"Thank you."

"What will you all have? It is my aim to serve you."

Xavier seemed to be oblivious to the attention.

"So Mira, may I offer you the buffet or a la carte?"

She looked into his eyes. He was not oblivious. Clearly sending a message to the server that he was unavailable. There was nothing going on between them, and yet he wanted the waitress to think there was.

"I was just thinking I wanted avocado toast, and bacon," Mira said nonchalantly.

"That sounds good to me. We'll have two. Thank you." He was very dismissive.

"Yes, Sir. Right away."

"Xavier, that was very rude of you!"

"Was I not to the point? There was nothing extra in my request for service, I will agree with you. And, I want to be clear, I am not to be fawned over as if I am some prize on the shelf."

"I guess you're right. You have a residence here, and I am sure they show deference to your desires."

"Believe me, I wouldn't know. I have only been here a few times in the last year. Mostly because my brother is visiting or my cousins who are also posted in America want to get away for a few days."

"Your family sounds very close."

"We are. It's my Tia and Tio's desire that all the cousins remain close, even though we long ago became adults.

"And do you all conform?"

"Si, very much so. We are all like brothers."

"Only male children?"

"Most of us are. There are a few girls, and not very close."

The waitress did not come back. Instead the chef delivered their meals personally.

"Mr. Gutiérrez, it is good to see you again. We hope you will find everything to be above standard."

"I am sure I will. May I present Ms. Mira Morales, a renowned business woman in her own right. She and I are having a business meeting here."

"Nice to meet you, Ms. Morales. Thank you for selecting our restaurant for your business meeting."

"It is nice to meet you Chef, and I very much appreciate your hospitality. It is a very lovely resort, and all the food I've had here has been very good."

"Kind of you to say that, ma'am. Are you staying here?"

"I am for a few days. I am a repeat offender as I have not found any other resort on this island with such great service."

"I will pass that onto management. Also, do you like chocolate?"

"Thank you! And yes, I very much so love chocolate."

"I will send up some truffles to your room. I have been experimenting with a new flavor."

"That is very kind of you."

"We value our customers and return visitors as well. Please do excuse me and enjoy your meal. If there is anything you need, do not hesitate to send for me."

Xavier spoke up. "Thank you, Chef!"

They watched as the head of the kitchen returned back the same way he had come.

"That was very nice."

"It definitely was. The chef found you charming."

"Me? He came over to speak to you. He didn't know me from Adam."

"Trust me Mira, he knows a beautiful woman when he sees one."

"Hmph, so you say. How about we actually commence our business meeting."

"Suit yourself. I'm ready."

Over breakfast, Mira shared her days' agenda with Xavier. It constituted of errands, meetings, and checking on equipment being shipped.

"No beach time?"

"Not for me and help yourself."

"I'm not one to sun bathe much."

"Me either."

"Not a beach lover?"

"Love is a strong word. I don't hate the beach. I just don't prefer it. I do love the view here though with its multiple hues of blue. And I'm always on the move so I have to catch my glimpses of the scenery as I go."

"You live at the beach back in Florida?"

"No, my home is several miles from the water."

"Surely the views of the Atlantic Ocean are as breathtaking as here?"

"They are a deeper shade of blue because they are colder. Not bad to look at, and my parents live in a coastal community so I grew up around water."

"Something to take for granted?"

"Perhaps so. I can go visit them anytime I want as they live off A1A. As I mentioned earlier, people take a lot of things for granted."

"I think I want to check out that area too. They say the city of St. Augustine has a chic, eclectic vibe. My Papa might be reminded of our home beaches in Costa del Sol."

"Yes, St. Augustine is a great place—with a rich history as the oldest established city in America. They have great restaurants, shops, schools, and many church denominations. You might even be able to find Sunday services in Spanish."

"Mira, you are sounding like a real estate agent."

"I doubt that. I have random facts picked up from living in the area, and listening to my parents' idle chatter."

"That is exactly what I need."

"Ummmhmmmm." She was not convinced.

"I definitely think a beach community will entice Papa to leave cold New York, even if only for the winter months."

"I get that you're not a fan of the NY experience."

"No, I'm definitely not. I went there out of work necessity, and temporarily moved Papa so I could watch over him in my comings and goings. I'm the most rational of his sons. Now that I've established a solid foundation for our family enterprise to grow, I want out of that area. I can't seem to get him to move. He has some new friends, who seem to want him to stay."

"You sound very protective of your father."

"I am. I believe Papa to be very charming. In the assisted living place, he has the women fighting over him."

"Oh wow!"

"Si! So you see, whatever we create has to be attractive. Quaint area...small beach town."

"You should check out the Gulf side too. There's Destin, Sandestin, Clearwater, Sarasota. Further down West Palm Beach, Ft. Lauderdale, Miami. All those areas get more hurricane impacts than Jacksonville and St. Augustine."

"The lowest part of Florida, maybe West Palm Beach. I've been many times to the Miami area. Too big and crowded. My dad would likely get himself in bigger trouble."

Mira wondered what he wasn't saying. She knew from her searching that Xavier had been photographed many times in Miami at rooftop parties, on the back of multi-million dollar yachts in St. Tropez and Monte Carlo, leaving night clubs in Milan, fancy parties in New York City. He was definitely a socialite! Was he purposefully looking for a quieter place to hide out? *Mira that's none of your business,* she admonished herself.

"Are you taking notes, doodling, or thinking?'

"Sorry, please repeat?"

He pointed to her note pad, that she on the table.
She'd been taking some preliminary notes as they
talked, and then had stopped writing after the word,
'no.'

"Oops sorry. I did get momentarily distracted."

"I was thinking of the beach towns on other coasts in
Florida." She hadn't outright lied. Miami is a beach
town. She scribbled big cities next to 'no.'

She closed her portfolio case, and looked back at
him.

"May I make a business request?"

"Of course. I can't promise I'll say yes."

"Gracias, Senorita." For the first time in her life, she
saw admiration in someone's eyes related to her
work—he was interested in her business!

"I'd love to tag along with you today, and see how
you work, if you don't mind?"

"I don't mind at all. It will help you see why I'm not
good at real estate."

"How did you get into your business niche market?"

"My parents spoiled me."

"How so?"

"I'm an only child. So they indulged me by taking me on great trips. It sparked my love of travel, and they told me I could be anything, do anything, go anywhere!"

"And you turned that into adventure tours?"

"Not at first. I tried a traditional office job. Hated it. I felt trapped at a desk."

"I know how that feels. So how did you get here?"

"Next, I tried a traditional travel agent. That lasted about four years. I worked for a top shelf business that catered to the rich and famous; retirees too with healthy bank accounts and time on their hands."

"Why did you leave?"

"People were too demanding and condescending. If you were coming to us, it was because we had the skills to assist. Most clients were often telling me how to do my job or complaining about the results when they didn't take our advice."

"That had to be frustrating."

"Not really. It just let me know I wanted something different. A new type of clients. All from referrals and who I could hand select."

"May I ask a personal question? Just one."

Mira wasn't sure how to answer that. Most of her clients or prospective clients didn't venture into the personal domain.

"Okay," she said nonchalantly picking up her coffee cup and taking a sip of fortitude.

"Are you married? Do you have children?"

"That's two questions." Mira was weary and yet not offended.

"You're right! And they still stand."

"Does it matter to our business dealings?"

"Not at all. I think what you've created is risky, gutsy, and fascinating all at the same time. I am curious how you juggle it and if there is a husband who supports you or children who also demand your attention."

"In that case, I do not mind responding. No husband or significant other. The business is definitely my baby. Any other personal questions?"

"Not at present."

Mira made a note on her pad. 'Remind client to stay focused.'

Chapter 6

"Life should not be a journey to the grave with the intention of arriving safely in a pretty and well preserved body, but rather to skid in broadside in a cloud of smoke, thoroughly used up, totally worn out, and loudly proclaiming, 'Wow! What a Ride!'"
~ Hunter S. Thompson, The Proud Highway: Saga of a Desperate Southern Gentleman

"I need to run an errand. Do you want to go or you want to stay here and sit on the beach?"

"You know I'm not a beach lubber."

"I do," she said tossing him a smile as she picked up her tote bag, and headed for the door.

He followed as she knew he would. She was impressed he didn't back down or question her before following her into her adventures. He didn't seem to be concerned with not having all the details. Most men wouldn't be so conciliatory.

The Jeep she'd rented would be waiting at valet when they got to the front. As they stepped into the main lobby of the *Ritz Carlton*, the concierge stepped forward to hand her the keys. She paused and Xavier stood close behind her, with his hand at the small of her back.

"Ms. Morales, the car is parked out front. I put some waters and a snack basket in the trunk."

"Remember, call me Mira, please. And thank you! Very kind of you Antonio! I love this level service!"

"A pleasure ma'am. You are very loyal staying here whenever you come through and we appreciate it."

"Your establishment is worthy of my loyalty!"

"I will leave you until your return."

"Have a great day," she waved as Antonio returned back to his desk.

"Will you drive?" she asked passing the key to Xavier.

"A pleasure ma'am," he leaned in to whisper in her ear.

She resisted pursing her lips together, and kept her nonchalant smile in place as she nodded. He was being possessive. She'd remain quiet. There was no threat here.

She willed herself to move the twenty feet forward out the glass doors that magically opened. Xavier held the door to the car open for her, and she hopped up and into the passenger seat. He closed it and walked around to the other side of the black vehicle, and slid in next to her.

"So where to?"

"Natural Bridge."

"What's that?"

"It's an area right along the ocean where people go to check out the view. It used to be a natural stone bridge above the ocean. Sadly the natural arch collapsed in 2005."

"How does this figure into your advance trip?"

"I have a group who's asked me to negotiate an overnight camping trip."

"That sounds cool."

"I hope so. I need to secure the deal."

"This camping trip must come with some complications."

"Yes, it's not a camp site. And it's highly restricted since the collapse."

"I'm sure you can persuade them."

"Money, and some good publicity might be attractive if it's controlled."

"Well give me the coordinates so I can put in the GPS."

She looked into her bag for the file, and provided the address. It was nice to have someone else along and to drive too. She could make some notes, stare out the window at the natural sights, and fill Xavier in on her plans.

When they arrived, he pulled into the car park. "Do you need me to come in with you?"

"No, I can handle it. I just wanted some company on the ride."

"It's pretty here, so I'm happy enough to wait for you here."

"Thanks! I appreciate it."

She picked up her bag, and escaped out the vehicle before he could come open her door. He was unnerving her. He was classy, kind and controlled with his power. And she felt like he respected her business acumen and the work she did. She shook her head. *Get into business mode*, Mira, she said to herself as she walked across the lot.

As she approached the small building that sat next to the snack shack, she spotted the door. Pulling it open, she walked in.

"What brings you to Aruba ma'am?"

"My name is Mira and I need to speak to someone about renting the place." She could see his name was Petro.

"We don't rent natural bridge. It's a natural geological rock formation."

"It's a tourist stop, right?"

"We have excursions like ATVs and bikes that ride on the grounds. People can walk around as long as they don't go onto the rocks."

"So it's for rent?"

"Well there are items available for rent on the facility, just not the grounds themselves. Unless you have an exception."

"Oh, so there are exceptions one could request, Petro?" Mira had gotten him to say more than their starting point.

"What did you have in mind?"

"I have a group of extreme hikers who want to camp out on the site."

"That's not going to be possible."

"Oh? Why not?"

"It's too dangerous and no one stays on the property overnight."

"What will it take to make that happen?"

"I'm sorry ma'am. There is no one who can help you."

"There is always someone. And I understand that you don't hold that power."

"It's not that I don't have power."

"I would never say that. It would be insulting to even imply that. My clients have their own podcast with millions of followers. They thought it would bring more fortune, the rights to a potential documentary with streaming, products and so forth if they were only able to capture the experience. It certainly did when they went on an overnight archaeological dig in Belize."

"It is highly unlikely your request would be allowed."

"Oh, so it's possible?"

"Yes, it could be. Let me speak with the interior minister and see what can be negotiated."

"Very well. I will be back tomorrow. I have a few more sights to check out as well. This one was first on their list; and if it doesn't work out, I am sure there will be other locales that will want the fame, notoriety and funding."

She politely got up from her seat, and dared not turn around. She knew she had said just enough for Petro to see dollar signs.

Mira walked back to the Jeep doing her best not to stare at Xavier, who was leaning against her side of the vehicle looking at the waves splash against the rocks.

"Done already? How did it go?"

"It went very well. They said come back tomorrow." She didn't elaborate. She knew her tactics often got people to listen and agree. And she'd be optimistic.

"You think it's beautiful here too. I can tell!"

"It's breathtaking! It's hard to see from here. I would imagine the tidal waves come in and are so unpredictable."

"There's more. Let me show you." She started walking towards the rocks. Xavier followed behind her, and they descended down the limestone gravel path. When they got to the bottom they could start to see where the bridge once stood.

"I would imagine this was some marvel before the collapse." He helped her climb up onto the rocks.

"I hear it was. I still think it's pretty. You see just over there, is Baby Bridge."

"I think this setting is spectacular! Thank you for showing it to me and letting me tag along."

"It was very nice to have some company. There are a number of beaches and hikes for day trips. My group wants to camp overnight."

"I am sure you will have it all work out."

"Thanks for the vote of confidence."

"Only calling it like I see it."

"Keys, please!" She put her hand out for the keys. He handed them over.

He still opened the driver's side door for her, and she put her bag over into the back before climbing in. In two steps he was back around to the passenger side.

"Seatbelt!"

"What? We going off road."

"Perhaps, and since this is rented to my company, I need to be responsible."

"Good point. I can take orders," he said smiling and clicking the belt.

"Somehow I doubt that. And I appreciate it." She backed up and turned back onto the rugged road. Off to the left and up the hill they road. Mira wanted to show him to a little seen spot on the island.

"Where are we going or is it a surprise?"

"I don't like surprises. I'm taking you to see *Blackstone Beach* and the *Indjueq Natural Triple Bridge.*"

"Sounds very interesting."

"You will see a hidden gem. It's rugged and desolate there, so we won't stay long."

"I'm game!"

The rest of the morning and early afternoon proved to be a fun adventure exploring Aruba, its beaches, and natural wonders. They'd even stopped for lunch at the popular *Salt and Pepper Restaurant*. There they discussed everything from popular tourist towns to futbol. Pulling back into the hotel's large circular driveway, Mira realized they'd been gone longer than she intended. As she'd pulled over to the side, the bellman must have sensed she was not quite ready to disembark from the vehicle.

"Sorry to keep you out all day," Mira apologized.

"Please, make no apologies. I had a great time!"

"Me too."

"Have I proven that we can work well together, and you will accept me as a client?"

"That's so not a fair question," she said trying to keep a straight face.

"Oh it is such a fair question! One I hope you will answer."

"Okay, yes Xavier. You win! I will take on the challenge of helping you find your next home."

"Excelente! What's next?"

"I will leave Aruba on Sunday. Let's plan to discuss my plan on Monday. Are you returning to New York? Spain?"

"No, I will plan to be in your office. I will call your assistant and get on your schedule."

"Thank you! As you are probably aware, my assistant keeps me on track."

"I kind of figured that to be the case. Any chance you want to have dinner?"

"Unfortunately, I have other plans."

"Understood! May I open the door for you?"

"Yes."

He jumped from the Jeep in a stealth move and came around to open her door for her; he helped her down. She left the keys in the ignition for the valet. As they walked to the doors, again they parted as if the sea had opened. Just inside the door, Xavier stopped.

"Thank you again for a great adventure, Aruba style! Until next time, Mira."

"A pleasure. Until then Xavier." With that he turned and walked away. It had been a perfect day. And Mira had so much work to do. She had enjoyed showing Xavier the unique places she'd discovered in Aruba. And she could kick herself for saying yes to taking him as a client. She just did not have the energy to resist. Truth be told, she had no desire to resist any longer. She would develop a plan, figure it out, and execute with no distractions. She hoped he wouldn't be the distraction.

Chapter 7

"As soon as I saw you, I knew a grand adventure was about to happen." ~ A. A. Milne

"I recommend Sandestin as a first stop. There's also Destin and 30A beach scene. All of it has an eclectic hip vibe, while still being a collection of beach towns."

"What's 30A?" Xavier asked as she drove them down the highway. They had landed by private jet at Destin Ft. Walton Beach Airport. He's rented a Jeep, noting it was a lucky car for them after their time in Aruba. That made Mira laugh.

"It's a Florida county road number. We are in the Panhandle and there are small beaches and towns that are very quaint. This area is sometimes called the *'Emerald Coast*;' at least until you get into Destin proper.

"Sounds a lot like the Costa del Sol."

"Tell me about it? I think you mentioned your father loved those beaches."

"The towns are built around the beaches, with lots of walking, small shops and eateries, families picnicking on the beach and having good times.

"It sounds very quaint, and comparable in this area. The Gulf has beautiful water. Probably as pretty as

Bermuda. As with every area, it has low-end, easy going restaurants and other upscale ones. Some specialize in local cuisine and others have an international fare. Nothing beats Gulf seafood!" She paused.

"This is good."

"I have four appointments for us to see houses this morning, and three for this afternoon. Most of them are either on the beach or within a couple of blocks."

"My Papa has never had a place directly on the beach. That might be good for his constitution."

"Each of the houses has at least two master bedrooms so you both will have every amenity."

"You've thought of everything! I really appreciate it."

"That's what you hired me to do."

"Si. Of course. How long until we get to the first house?"

"We're almost there. Five minutes more. It's right on 30A, West County Highway."

Mira hoped he liked the houses she had selected. He hadn't really had much criteria. Six bedroom, six bathrooms. Near the beach, with enough space for himself, his father, and his cousins.

She pulled in front of a two garage house, and cut the engine. "Ready."

"Si."

She jumped down from the vehicle and met him on the other side.

"This house has a lot of steps up. Just as you asked, six bedrooms, six bathrooms."

"Those are a lot of steps."

"Yes. And it is said to have breathtaking views, a private pool, its own beach walkway, and a carriage house." He followed her up the steps. She put in the code on the lockbox, and the door opened up.

"That is a great view," he said as they made their way to the living room at the back of the house.

"The *Gulf of Mexico* is very warm, and hence the beautiful hues of water."

"No complaints here."

The rest of the morning went by in a blur. Mira drove them to *Pescado Rooftop Restaurant* at *Rosemary Beach*. It was a good break from the looking at houses. After ordering her lunch, and watching Xavier order his, she thought it best to make notes.

"The houses later today will be closer to Destin. Destin, while maybe it doesn't have the same level of beach as Sandestin, it does have other charms."

Don't you feel it?"

"Feel what?" She asked, clearly confused how the conversation had shifted from talking about places to stay on the gulf coast of Florida.

"Come now Mira. Don't play me as a fool."

She bit her tongue ready to challenge his smug attitude. Just wait. He'll break the silence. She chewed on the end of her pencil and watched him.

"You and I have an attraction to each other."

"Really?"

"Yes really! How do you feel about that?"

She pondered her next words very carefully. "Well, if that were indeed the case, and it's not, then it would be inappropriate."

"I beg to differ. We are both adults."

"Might I speak frankly?"

"I'd have it no other way."

"Remember you hired me to work with you to find a new home here in Florida, or Puerto Rico, or Bermuda. I arrange high-end trips. I don't get involved with my clients. Regardless of whether you feel we have an attraction, I won't cross the line."

"What would it take?"

"For what?" She was clearly losing her practiced patience.

"For you to consider dating me?"

"You're an international playboy, Mr. Gutiérrez. There are a fleet of women who have and continue to want to date you. I am not interested. A wise woman once told me don't take sand to the beach."

"You've done your research on me, I see. Intriguing."

"I'm thorough. And I get my job done."

"Did you research my cousin too as part of arranging his travel."

"No."

"Why am so special?"

"Your cousin didn't summon me to Spain with twenty-four hours of notice. Matter of fact, he didn't summon me anywhere. He simply said over the phone he wanted to hire me to coordinate a spectacular honeymoon. And I did."

"Yes, the happy couple raved of their time away.

Back to you. I find you intriguing. Challenging, equally beautiful and dismissive.”

“Could we please refocus on discussing Florida?”

“I’d fire you if I thought it would end our business relationship and further our personal one. But for now, I think it’s best I let you do your job.”

Clearly he was not listening. She would not be unnerved.

“Look, you’re not doing me any favors. I didn’t have to take you on as a client. Please don’t make me regret it.”

“You win. I will drop the topic. At least for today.”

“Excellent. Back to the subject at hand.”

Nothing more came up for the rest of the afternoon regarding any attraction they might have for each other. Mira was relieved because she did find Xavier Gutiérrez attractive—and equally off-limits.

Chapter 8

"Life is full of surprises, but the biggest one of all is learning what it takes to handle them."
~ Deborah Wiles

"Hi Mira! How's it going with the next phase of houses."

"Hi Xavier. It's good. I know you didn't end up liking the Gulf Coast."

"It was okay. The houses were beautiful. I am just not sure Papa would like it there."

"There's plenty of places still left to show you. I have found a list of homes in Jacksonville near *Atlantic Beach* and *Neptune Beach*; then others along A1A in *Ponte Vedra* and then down into St. Augustine.

"Sounds like more small beach towns?"

"They're somewhat different because they are Atlantic Ocean, not Gulf. The surf is more aggressive, and the views bluer."

"I will defer to your expertise."

"Ummmhmmmm. When are you available to return to Florida?"

"Next week. You around then?"

"I can be. Where are you now?"

"I just arrived back to Europe. I'm visiting my cousins. We're going to see the *Champions League* futbol match in Paris. You all call it *Champions League Soccer* in the States."

"Sounds like a fun time!"

"Si, I suppose so. A bunch of grown men pretending like we are young again. I'd rather be looking at houses with you."

"I don't believe that! Not one bit."

"I wouldn't lie to you. Sometimes hanging out with my cousins can be too much."

"Too much?"

"Too much testosterone. It's a couple of days, so I'll adjust."

"Well, I will let you go, so you can get back to it."

"Mira?"

"Yes?"

"Send through our plans. The sooner I find a house, the sooner I can end this stalemate between us, and ask you out."

"Bye Xavier." She dropped the line, smiling to herself. He was incorrigible.

Miguel walked through the door and plopped down in her chair.

"Didn't you promise to send me Senor Gutiérrez's schedule?"

"Yes, I just needed to get his availability before I sent it to you to schedule."

"You talked to him?"

"Yes, I just got off the phone with him."

"No fair. I thought you said I could reach out to him."

"Miguel, he is not gay!"

"How do you know?"

"Well let me say, I don't think he's gay."

"How do you know, Mira?"

"He asked me out."

"He did? When? Why didn't you tell me? I want dets!" Miguel bolted upright like a dog begging for a bone.

“There is nothing to tell. I don’t mix work and pleasure. I told him I’m not interested.”

“Wait, you turned him down? You’re not interested? Why would you turn down such an amazing find…accent and all?”

“Miguel, you are not listening to me. I don’t mix business and pleasure!”

“If you don’t want him, can I ask him out?”

“No Miguel, you cannot.”

“Oh, so you are attracted to him!”

“He’s alright.”

“Mira, Mira on the wall, please don’t ignore his call. If you simply give in and say yes, then you can have it all!”

Mira laughed. “Miguel, you are too much! Now back to work pullleeeeeeeeaaaazzzzzzzz.”

“Okay, suit yourself. And just know, I will take your leftovers.”

“Out of my office! Out, out, out…” She could hear him laughing as he sauntered across her office and out through the doorway he had come from.

Mira spun around in her chair. What if Miguel was right? Could she have it all? Not with a playboy

who just wanted her to be the flavor of the week. Or
the month. She wasn't interested in that type.

****

Three Days Later…

 Mira typed Xavier's name into the internet search.
A recent photo from the night before popped up
under news. *"The Playboy Cousins are back at it!"*
She could see them coming out of a Paris nightclub.
Xavier had a woman on each arm. In front of him
was another man, called Tomas Miguel Gutiérrez,
which Mira assumed was a cousin since they shared
the same last name.

*See Xavier, you are proving to me exactly why you
are not a man I can go out with,* she said aloud.
Disgusted that she had started to lower her guard with
him, she closed the window and her laptop. She was
so glad she had seen the article in the nick of time.
She needed to hurry up and get this assignment
complete so she could go back to her life, and forget
Xavier Gutiérrez ever existed.

Chapter 9

My point is that you do not need me or anyone else around to bring this new kind of light in your life. It is simply waiting out there for you to grasp it, and all you have to do is reach for it. The only person you are fighting is yourself and your stubbornness to engage in new circumstances.
~ Jon Krakauer, Into the Wild

Mira had agreed to meet Xavier for lunch in *Jax Beach* before their afternoon of house hunting. It was better to have neutral ground, she'd decided. There was a lovely, laid back restaurant called *Land Shark Bar and Grill* in the *Margaritaville Hotel.* Mira was taken with the idea that Xavier was a shark acting harmless with her. Yet, she wasn't a heartbroken conquest. As she pulled into a lucky front spot, she gathered her bag. She could see him strolling up the steps dressed in casual navy slacks and matching pullover shirt. His hair lightly blowing in the breezes coming off the Atlantic Ocean. He looked delicious and Mira wasn't exactly hungry; at least not for food. No one should have such good looks and charisma. It was a dangerous combination.

Get a grip woman….get out of the car, and go handle your business. Remember, business? That's why you're here. She shook her head to clear her mind.

She stepped down onto the sidewalk, and crossed to the same steps he had just ascended. At she reached the top, he must have seen her, as he swung open the glass doors.

"Mira, it is so good to see you again," he said in his thick Spanish accent. Through the doorway, she stopped and turned towards him, catching a whiff of his vanilla cedar cologne.

"Hello Xavier. Welcome back to Florida!"

"Gracias, querida."

"Dear?"

"Perdón Mira. A term of endearment for friends."

"A language thing. I do get it. It's good to meet. Let's get a table."

"Si, of course."

"The hostess showed them to a table out on the patio with a view of *Jax Beach* and the ocean."

"It's beautiful here too. A sunny day with temperatures in the mid-eighties in Fall."

"I agree. Of course I grew up on the Atlantic side of Florida. So, I'm biased. We have sunrise in the East and they have sunset on the Gulf."

"I would love to see sunrise on the water every day."

"Well then, you should think about these houses we will see this afternoon. Perhaps one of them will be the one."

"Sir. Ma'am, would you like to order? The drink menu is here, and the food in the one behind." A young waiter said interrupting their chatter.

"Will you give us a minute?" Mira politely asked.

"Yes, I will be back," he said and then disappeared.

"Let's order so we stay on schedule?"

Xavier let her order first. She selected a club sandwich and side salad. He ordered a cheeseburger and fries. They were such opposites.

"Tell me about the houses?"

Mira told him all the details of the houses. Most of them were in Ponte Vedra, a more exclusive area on this side of Florida. Some on the ocean, and others with waterfronts, piers and access to the ocean. After lunch was over, she got the check.

"Ready?" She said after signing the receipt.

"Si, lead the way," offering her to go ahead of him.

Outside at curbside, he asked, "Who's driving?"

"This time, how about you drive?"

"You don't have to ask me twice. I like being in control."

"About that, I have no doubt."

"And Mira, whether I find a house today or not, either way, you're fired!"

"What are you talking about? You haven't even seen Bermuda and Puerto Rico."

"Who cares! I'm sure I'll find something in Florida!"

"What about the game plan?"

"I've grown weary of fighting my attraction to you. I desire an us."

"Xavier, that sounds like fantasy talk!"

"I desire you. That's real! You're real! Let's see where this can go?"

"No!"

"Why not?"

"Didn't you spend all this effort to convince me to help you find a Southern home."

"Si. And you've helped me do that. I can be satisfied that you provided me with amazing service."

"We're standing in the middle of a sidewalk, and you're firing me."

"Not exactly. I just want you to hear me!"

"I hear you!"

"Tell me how you feel?"

"Feelings? You want to talk about my feelings?"

"Si!"

"I'm frustrated with you!"

"What did I do?"

"You just want your way, and damn everything else. That's impulsive!"

"I can understand this sentiment."

"I don't even understand. Can we just go get in the car? I live in this area and I don't want to have all my business becoming community conversation."

"Of course."

"Why are you so amenable about some things, and not others?"

"I'm trying to give you some of what you want."

"Really?"

"Si, my rental car is just over there. Let us go."

She put one foot in front of the other, and followed him to the car. He opened the passenger side door for her, and she slid into the candy red, *Corvette*. He closed her door and went to his side, effortlessly sliding in.

"Mira, I realize that perhaps we should table this conversation until after our house tour."

"Oh now you want to get back on schedule."

"Si. And I promise as soon as we've seen the last house today, we can return back to this conversation."

"Okay fine!"

"Here's my phone. Please load the first address."

She did as he asked, and so began their day of house hunting.

Chapter 10

"Some of our important choices have a time line. If we delay a decision, the opportunity is gone forever. Sometimes our doubts keep us from making a choice that involves change. Thus an opportunity may be missed." ~ James E. Faust

"I can't believe you found "the house." Mira said as they sat parked next to her car. They'd made it back to where they started six hours earlier.

"Me either. I will have my lawyers make an offer."

"I'm sure you will be successful. The listing agent seemed quite taken with you."

"Are you jealous?"

'Not at all! Even with our business complete, dating you is off the table."

"Stop with making the excuses."

"It's not an excuse. It goes with your reputation."

"What reputation are you referring?"

Mira shrugged her shoulders, being as cool as she could feign.

"Mira, what do you think you know about me?"

"That you're a playboy who wines and dines women all over the world!"

"Don't believe everything you read Mira."

"You were in Paris, supposedly for soccer with your cousins? It seems like you were out partying all night."

"I was in Paris at the soccer matches with my cousins."

"Are you saying that you weren't there at the clubs too?"

"No. I'm not saying that. How I was characterized isn't exactly the truth. I was there to help my cousin."

"Really? You read the articles."

"Si really!" He exhaled and continued. "My cousin Tomas Miguel is the playboy. As soon as those articles run, we are informed. The company has a media department with lots of high powered lawyers who get paid to find these very articles."

"Yes, the other male with you had the same last name. But both of you were surrounded by women. Clearly they were not cousins!"

"Yes, part of TM's entourage of so called friends. We were leaving and they were hanging on looking for an after party. Once we were out of the public eye, they went on their way. I took TM back to our apartment, alone. The newspapers are never going to print that."

"Look, you seem like a really great guy…"

“That has been said about me in the past.”

“Yes, well I guess it depends on who you ask.”

“I suppose it would.”

“You’re not going to plead your case that you are a nice guy? Misunderstood? Characterized in an unfavorable light?”

“Mira, I think I heard you say you checked my references right after you took my first phone call.”

“Yes, well that was for business. Dating you would be different.”

“Those who vouched for me as a client, they are the ones who know me better than anyone.”

“Wouldn’t they lie for you?”

“In my family, there is honor in telling the truth, not lying. Even if I was misunderstood, characterized in an unfavorable light, if I was as you say, as they say, I would never lie.”

“It’s admirable you are honorable and willing to be responsible for your actions, especially these days.”

“There is only one way to find out if I am honorable or not. And that is to discover for yourself.”

“You make it sound so easy.”

"It is very easy. I'm here. You're here. Business is not in our way anymore. I like that you're not willing to just go along to get along. You're beautiful, fun, unpretentious and generous! Also, you have to admit, we enjoy each other's company."

"Oh you're just trying to sway me with your charm."

"I am. Is it working?"

"Maybe, a little," she giggled. "I am not used such attention."

"Perhaps you should be."

"What do you mean?"

"A man should cater to the woman he wants. Not just to get her. But to keep her. If a man isn't into you, he won't treasure you. If he treasures you in the beginning, and that ceases to continue, then it's time to let the relationship go. People shouldn't stay together and be miserable."

"You have experience with that too?"

"Si. Unfortunately. Men move on a lot easier than women. It is how males are raised."

"That's awful!"

"It's the nature of hormones and the chase. If he values his family and he brings you home, then he's serious. If he refuses to incorporate you into his life, then he is just with you until the next best thing comes along.”

“Is that just Spanish men?”

“I doubt it and I have little knowledge of other cultures to prove otherwise.”

“I’ve never considered that view, even across the animal species.”

“No matter. We’ve all done things we are not proud of Mira.”

“I know. But still.”

“That’s not our case. I see you and how special you are! You are the woman I want. For me. I don’t give a damn about the past, mine or yours!”

“You are certainly direct!”

“I will not lie and pretend. Not my nature.”

“I don’t know about tomorrow Xavier. How about just for today, we celebrate that you found a house where you and your father will prosper?”

“You found us a house.”

“Word semantics. You know what I mean.”

“Si, si. On one condition. Have dinner with me? I have to return to New York tomorrow.”

"No, not tonight. I need to process all of this."

"Bueno. I will be back in two weeks. Let's make a date, even if you don't call it a date? These weeks will give you lots of time to further investigate me, and consider if you are interested in an us, work aside."

"Deal, dinner in two weeks! No need to call it a date," she said smiling. She could see aliveness in his eyes for the first time since they started this conversation.

"You're saying yes. Si?"

"Si. I agree!"

"Excelente!"

"Have a good night and safe trip Xavier," she said opening the car door and jumping out before he could do the gentlemanly thing. This conversation had been awkward for her. The more distance she could put between them, the more time she had to rebuild the wall around her emotions.

"Buenas noches querida," was all he said. He looked very satisfied with himself.

She pushed the Corvette's door closed, and turned to walk the ten steps to her car. She was unsteady on her feet, and felt like the impasse between her business sense and her heart had just been settled. She hadn't seen this coming before she met this man, with his debonair charm, good looks, and alluring personality. If she had, then she would not have taken the call. Had Mira just gotten herself into a whole new world of trouble? One way or another, she'd find out soon enough as two weeks was just around the corner…

Chapter 11

"It's so empowering to say, "This isn't serving me"
and walk away in peace."
~ Author Unknown

Just out of the meeting finalizing the legal details of the house sale with their lawyer, Sherlene, and his cousin Bertram, Xavier turned in his chair. The Manhattan skyline over the East River never disappoints. He loved this location in Lower Manhattan on Water Street, with floor to ceiling glass panels. Yet, he was ready for something new. Oceanfront property would bring a different perspective on nature not crafted in metal and concrete. He loosened his tie, unbuttoning the collar of his lucky blue shirt. End of the day. Xavier hoped to convince Papa to come stay too, at least part-time. It was a short flight of less than three hours into Jacksonville. He knew neither of them would permanently be relocating. The family interests in business were still primary to be ran out of these NY offices. And Papa had created a good existence finally. His private office phone rang. He pressed the speakerphone button.

"Hello!" He was in America so he answered in the customary greeting.

"I want you back!" He knew that voice. It was Dana.

"No!"

"Come on Xa. I was hasty in ending our relationship."

"I now know you were right. You deserve someone who can commit to you."

"Yes. You!"

"No Dana, I'm not for you."

"We can try again!"

"I don't think so. Goodbye Dana." He pressed the same button again dropping the line.

Xavier had no patience for Dana's indecisiveness and since it was forever over with her, he was more than ready to focus on Mira. This new possibility might not have occurred to him if Dana hadn't splashed cold water on his psyche a few weeks ago. Now that she was in his past, and he'd found a new house in Florida, he could focus on the here and now. And he needed to figure out how to get Mira to say yes to go out with him again after their upcoming dinner date. That was his number one priority.

Two days later...

Xavier walked into his NY apartment. It had been a long day of business meetings, and he still had one more event tonight—a cigar party on the *Upper East Side*. Inside the doorway, he could see in front of him stood his former fling, in his living room dressed in his bath robe, and holding a glass of wine.

"Dana, what are you doing here?"

"Hello darling!"

"Let me repeat, what are you doing here?"

"I used the key you gave me and let myself in. I made dinner."

"I have plans. You have to go." He walked over to his wet bar, and made a drink. Scotch, neat.

"You just got home. I was serious when I said I want you back, Xa!"

He didn't immediately respond. Instead choosing to consume some of the liquor. Smooth going down, unlike his current mood.

"Dana, let me be clear. I was serious when I said no."

"Can't we talk about it?"

"There's nothing more to say!"

"I think there is. We were good together."

"I'm leaving. Have your dinner! Get dressed, and leave my key on the table when you go!" He paused to drink the rest of the liquid. "You know what, you can keep the key as a souvenir because I will be having the locks changed, and telling reception to deny you access going forward."

"I get you are upset with me! How about we make up in the bedroom? Dinner will keep."

"No, that is never happening again. Goodbye Dana!"

He walked out the door he had literally just entered. Dana had been a distraction that he could no longer afford, especially now that he might have met the woman of his dreams, literally and figuratively. What he had said to Mira was true—she was the type of woman one could proudly take home to meet the family.

Chapter 12

"My life is proof that no matter what situation you're in, as long as you have a supportive family, you can achieve anything." ~ Michaela DePrince

"Papa, I've acquired another place." Xavier entered the sunroom at his father's "assisted" living facility.

His father looked up from the newspaper he was reading while sipping on his morning cafe.

"Where this time? Don't you get tired of acquiring new homes?" He knew his father hated his last acquisition, that apartment in New York. He said it was a concrete jungle, devoid of fresh air and sea breezes.

"This one is along the ocean just south of Jacksonville, Florida. "

"It's on what ocean?" His father perked up.

"The Atlantic. In the southern United States. It's not quite Costa del Sol, and I think you'll like it."

"Me?"

"Si, Papa. I got it with you in mind. It will be our winter home with warm breezes when it's cold here and back in Jaen too. Summers will be hot there, and I'm told there's always a breeze."

"Come, hijo. Sit. I want to hear more." Papa set aside his newspaper.

For the first time in a long while, Xavier could see his father was interested in something. Losing Mama all those years back had been devastating. They said his mother had a mild-mannered personality. Yet she was a determined woman and brought life to their family. Papa said she helped him stay calm and peaceful, and they did everything together: daily trips to the market, weekly walks by the seaside; they danced at fiestas, attended church together before taking a long Sunday drive. On many occasions he'd overheard Tia Catherine say that since her death, Papa's spark of a *'joie de vie'* was gone. Papa only had left the property for family events he could not escape attending. The move into this facility in New York was meant to get Papa away from those memories and bring him back to life. Xavier was surprised he'd said yes to him when Xavier announced he needed to move to America to support the family business operation. He still remembered that conversation. He'd been in the kitchen of his youth.

> *Papa was at the square kitchen table, in his usual spot on the wood chair that symbolized his place. Xavier sat in his space, to the left of his dad. The woven seat still held his weight even though he was now a grown man who whose feet touched the floor in what once was an impossible dream. The morning sun poured in the windows located above the porcelain sink cascading prisms of light that*

*filled the room with brightness and warmth—
it was a scene that symbolized love. He'd
rarely came there, preferring to see his dad
outside of that house. It was plagued with
ghosts of family fun times overshadowed with
his father's grief and sadness.*

*His brother, Matias, was now living mostly
full-time in Monaco, and he split his time
between his apartment in town and a myriad
of others throughout the world. He'd failed at
getting Papa to move to Monte Carlo. Both
he and his brother had preferred apartments
over single-family homes that required
maintenance and upkeep. He'd said yes so
fast it shocked him. And then as if he'd made
up his mind, he requested Xavier immediately
drive him to the estate so he could his Tio
Antonio and Tia Catherine. Papa was
alluding to his cousins' Gutierrez estate,
where they grew olives and ran all the
production of olive oil for their family
business. Xavier watched his dad drink the
last of the contents in his cup, get up from the
table, and set the cup in the sink. He stood a
little taller, moved with purpose, and had
started to hum. This just might make a
difference in his quality of life. No one could
replace Mama in their father's heart. And
even though Xavier had no memory of his
mother, he suspected she would be distraught
to see her beloved wasting away in this house
that was never meant to be a mausoleum.*

"Hijo, I'm waiting." Xavier had gone off into his own memories of the past.

"Of course Papa. You're going to love it. The nearby towns remind me of our family trips to Benalmadena.

"Does it sit on the ocean proper?" Papa's voice again cut into his reminiscent longings of childhood.

"Si, it does. It has six bedrooms, seven toilets and an open design to let in natural light from all angles. Two upper levels, each with three bedrooms and yours on the main level. You have your own ocean view and balcony. You won't have to be bothered by the impact of steps on your knees."

Tia Catherine was right, when she suggested to him the brilliant idea of finding a warm beach place to get Papa out of his funk. She reminded Xavier of all the great times he and his cousins had along the Mediterranean coast in summers gone by. The adults would watch over their antics and mischief, letting boys be boys.

"It sounds like a mansion."

"Not really. More of a cottage layout with lots of space for family to visit. I would rather not share our bedrooms or put family up in a hotel when they come spend time with us."

"Ah si. We are many. And one day when you take a wife and have children, they will fill that house with laughter."

"Let's not get ahead if ourselves Papa. It's a house of men: you, me, my brother and extended family on occasion."

"One day, mi hijo the right one will come and capture your heart. It will be like a demon has taken over suppressing all logical thought. All you will want is to be with her, watch the sun and moon rise, and set on her every look. It was like that with your Mama. I could barely look away."

"I'm not sure I want that kind of obsession." Quiet as it was kept, Mira was driving him crazy with her matter of fact personality and stone wall refusing to let him into her world. Was she one who could sway him to obsession? He was not going to kill himself trying to date her. After all there were plenty of other fish in the sea. And he definitely was not looking for an obsession.

"You will relish it when it happens. I see it in your cousins who have taken wives. They are having amazing adventures steeped in love. I am sad without your mother, and yet I know she loved me passionately until the day she died; I will forever be devoted to her. Not a minute goes by when I don't miss her."

"Me too, Papa. She would have loved the idea of spending winters in a warmer climate. I doubt she would have left our house though."

"Perhaps not. She could be stubborn."

"We will always keep the homeplace too, Papa."

"Si. With these mostly gloomy days, I could use some seaside sun and warm temperatures. When can I see this American beach cottage?"

"In a few weeks. It is getting repainted. I want to make sure it's perfect for my Papa!"

"I am excited. Maybe Catherine and Antonio will come visit. Here is not a good visit for them. Ocean and warmth might be just the idea to get them to America."

"I am sure you will tell them all about it. And once you're settled, we'll make plans for them to come."

"Yes, I will call them tomorrow and tell them the news."

"Bueno. I will be back pronto. I have to go back to Florida. Is there anything that I can do for you."

"No. This place is fine. I am doing fine. I am looking forward to being on the Atlantic Ocean. Remember the walks Mama and I used to take on the beach?"

"I don't Papa. I was too young. You always said those were good times."

"Si. Oh well. Time for me to return back to my newspaper."

"Have a good week Papa." Xavier knew that the memory of his mother was enough to send his father's spirits back down. When it was like that, then Papa wanted to be alone.

"I will. You too, my son."

Xavier rose and placed a kiss on his father's head. For now. He was satisfied that his latest endeavors to find the perfect place to give Papa a new outlook was paying off. He owed the credit to Mira who painstakingly found viable choices before they came onto the market. Even though she was not into real estate, she knew how to use her connections. He would have to provide a bonus for exceeding his expectations. Life was indeed looking up for both him and his father!

Chapter 13

"The purpose of life is to live it, to taste experience to the utmost, to reach out eagerly and without fear for newer and richer experience." ~ Eleanor Roosevelt

"I'm close. I made second place in Sao Paolo. Brazil!" Mira could hear the excitement in her friend, Lella's voice.

"So I heard. Congrats my friend! Sorry I missed it. Work has been crazy busy." Mira said over the phone line.

"Will you come to my race in Las Vegas next week? I'll send a flight ticket. I have a room for you."

"Ummm I have plans." Lella was a *Formula One* race driver—actually the first woman racer on the circuit with the men in decades.

"Change them. I really want you in the grandstand cheering me on and to be there when I accomplish world dominance."

"You deserve it! And I can't."

"So who is he?"

"How do you know it's a he?"

"Because you're not forthcoming. If you had to work, you would've said it. So who is he?"

"It's early yet. Just a couple of interactions. He's a former client."

"What? He must be special as you never mix business and pleasure."

"I said former client. I was a no. And he's so alluring that he seems to be wearing down my resistance."

"I have an idea. Bring him along. I have plenty of resources at my disposal. I'm at the top of my game and my team sponsor is rolling out the red carpet."

"I don't think that would send the right signal."

"Mira, it's a race, not an orgy. It's not even halfway around the world, since it's in America."

"Yeah you're definitely not far from Florida when you race in Miami, Houston and Vegas."

"Just come, please! You know I wouldn't ask if I didn't need you here. I trust you and I need support to make my final push in this male dominated sport!"

She sighed. Lella was right. She rarely asked for anything.

"Okay I'll come. I'll think about whether to include Xavier."

"Oh thank you my best all-around shero! I'll email plane tickets, add your name plus guest to be all access, including VIP race and party lists. You know how to get into my apartment. Anything I've forgotten?"

"Nope, you've got it covered."

"I'll be going into radio silence, race mode in five days. You know how to get in touch with me or Ricardo if you need anything."

She knew Ricardo was Lella's agent. "Yes I do. Don't worry about me. I'll be there with or without Xavier."

"I do like that name…"

"Don't you have some laps to run," she said purposefully cutting her friend off. Mira could hear laughter as the line dropped.

What a mess! She'd have to postpone the ride down coastal A1A she'd promised Xavier for their dinner. That wasn't as troublesome as the idea him going with her to Las Vegas. She wouldn't miss out though on supporting the best friend she'd ever had.

****

"Hello Bella Mira!" She was unsure how to respond to Xavier addressing her as beautiful. She'd ignore it.

"Hi! I know we had made plans next week and I need to change them. Actually postpone them."

"Oh you have cold feet?"

117

"Not at all. I have to go to Las Vegas."

"A new client?"

"Nope, an old one of sorts. My once client and now good friend Lella is racing on the *Formula One* circuit and I've been summoned to her *Las Vegas Grand Prix* race next week."

"You're friends with Lella Rossi?"

"Yes, you know of her?"

"Si. She's the best formula driver in the last few years, regardless of being a female. She is on the verge of breaking through and perhaps on next year's circuit, she will take it all."

"I'm impressed!"

"Oh you think I'm am not well versed in many subjects, si?"

"No, I wouldn't say that. Anyway would it be okay to change the plan?"

"Of course. I'm disappointed and I understand. I'd choose cheering my friend in Grand Prix over spending time with me too."

"Well she asked me to bring you with me."

"Wow, she did?"

"Yes. I explained we had dinner plans. Instead, she's sending plane tickets, and is adding our names to the VIP race and party lists. You wanna come with me?"

"A thousand yesses! Of course I will go!"

"Okay I'll send more details when I get the email."

"Great. Did I mention my brother has a place in Las Vegas? While he mostly lives in Monte Carlo, he picked up a condo in Vegas because he likes to gamble."

"Where? Wait, you did say you have a brother!"

"Si I have a brother. His name is Matias. He mostly lives in Monte Carlo. Just like me, he has numerous residences around the world. He works for the company too. And he is a huge *Formula One* fan. I wonder if he will be in Vegas that week."

"That seems so random that your brother might be there. Anyway, I will get back to you."

"Thanks Mira for keeping your promise to see me next week."

"Of course. I'm looking forward to it…" With that she dropped the line, not wanting to give Xavier a chance to respond.

Chapter 14

"Travel and tell no one, live a true love story and tell no one, live happily and tell no one, people ruin beautiful things." ~ Kahlil Gibran

The following Wednesday, Mira and Xavier flew into Las Vegas' *Harry Reid International Airport* on commercial jet. As promised, Lella had arranged all the details. Lella owned a three-bedroom condominium on the *Las Vegas Strip*. They had been picked up in the arrivals area by a chauffeur driven car, and whisked off to get settled in before going to the track. As they road along past the familiar hotels such as *MGM Casino, New York, New York, Caesar's Palace, Paris, the Bellagio, the Venetian, the Wynn*, Mira couldn't help but wonder how the city had been transformed into a race track. Already up was lots of fencing. Yet, cars were still on the streets as if they had no idea a race was coming. She knew from attending a few other races that track races were a whole different beast.

"I have never been here during race week. Looks like lots of preparations are under way." Xavier spoke the words as if he was in her thoughts.

"I haven't either. I've had the opportunity to go to other cities for the *Formula One* circuit, and many of those races are on a track, not the street. This is impressive!"

"I imagine we haven't seen the half of it?"

"True. Were you able to get in touch with your brother?"

"Yes, he arrived two days ago. Thank you for getting him a ticket for our itinerary."

"Oh of course. Lella has all kind of benefits."

"Well she's a star, so the seas should part for her."

"Agreed. She said she won't be staying at the condo. They have them in seclusion and on a tight schedule. We can get settled in, and then go to the race paddock or you can meet up with your brother and I will go alone."

"I'm going with you."

"Don't you want to spend some time with your brother?" Mira was curious about his relationship with a brother. As an only child, she'd longed for a sibling her entire childhood. It just never happened.

"Absolutely not. I will see him tomorrow at the practice day one."

"Still, you've come a long way."

"Are you trying to get rid of me?"

"No, just trying to be polite."

"I see my brother often. He would not even have rearranged life to see me on this trip, if not for me mentioning VIP access and Lella."

"Oh?"

"Yes, he is obsessed with the F1 circuit. He typically gets tickets to their events as they traipse around the globe. This time though, it includes an introduction to the hottest racer about to emerge to the champions level. He returned my call."

"Are you two not very close?"

"We are, just there is an age difference of four years. I'm in the younger set of cousins and he is closer to the older ones."

"Well, I'm glad that he will get to be with us, especially if he is a fan."

"Two Gutiérrez brothers might be too much, and at least it is not all of us!"

"From what you've told me, it sounds like there's lots of fun and laughter amongst you all."

"Very much so. And baby steps. Plus, I don't want any competition. I found you first!"

"Well actually it was Valentino who found me," she pointed out diplomatically.

"That doesn't count, he's off the market. Perhaps tonight, we can have our dinner date."

"Are you trying to stake your claim before I am swayed by anyone else?" Mira could barely keep a straight face.

"Si. I'm not sharing you with any other males. At least not until I have you devoted to me."

"You are hysterical!"

"You did promise me dinner!"

"Dinner in Vegas sounds wonderful."

The driver pulled into a circular driveway, and stopped at the glass entrance. Before she knew what had happened, they had been whisked into the lobby, and up to Lella's condo. Security didn't seem to be an issue, even though one of the most famous people on the planet was in residence. She and Xavier put their stuff in separate guest bedrooms, and met back in the living room.

"Ready to go? Lella said the same driver would wait for us, to take us to the secured area."

"Si. Let's go!"

Chapter 15

"The biggest adventure you can ever take is to live the life of your dreams." ~ Oprah Winfrey

Behind the famed *Las Vegas Strip* was a parking lot that catered to those who had access to *F1 Racing's* most exclusive members. With VIP passes, Mira and Xavier had been able to get within a block of the *Paddock Club* after the driver dropped them off. Lella had left laminated passes that they were told to put on before they departed the car. Membership had its privileges.

"Lella said follow the signs for *Mercedes* Team Garage." Mira noted as she read the email instructions on her cell.

"It's over there." Xavier pointed.

"I think Lella plans for us to be in the *Paddock Club* suites, where closest relatives and guests of the teams are located. There we should be able to see the driver pits, the start and finish line."

"Wow, that is fantastic! It's like being a kid in the candy store. I will do my best not to drool being so close to the track."

"Yes, do try to contain yourself," Mira laughed.

As they walked up to the garage zone, they could see lots of activity preparing for practice days. Mira knew there were interviews, commentaries, and of course lots of speculation.

"Mira, Mira, over here!" She heard her friend call out using her pet name. She waved.

When she had reached the front of the garage she could see Lella already checking out Xavier, with speculative eyes.

"You made it! I am so glad." They hugged.

"I wouldn't miss it for anything. Thank you for the tickets, use of your condo, and the driver."

"A pleasure. Now who is this? My name is Lella." She reached out her hand to Xavier.

"Lella Rossi, it is an honor to meet you. I'm Xavier Gutiérrez, one of your biggest fans!" He shook her hand.

"Charming, he is!" Lella said turning briefly to Mira. Then turning back to him, she continued, "It's nice to meet you. Make sure you're good to my bestie, Mira, or else you'll have me to contend with."

"You're not only skilled in a racing, you are direct too. I like it! I'm harmless, and I promise that I have only the best intentions with Mira."

Mira cleared her throat. "Excuse me, you two. I am standing right here. I can take care of myself."

Lella hugged her friend again. "No doubt. Now let me give you all the quick tour. I only have a few minutes. However, you have access to everything. There is a spread of food upstairs."

"We only came to see you and wish you the luck you don't need! Win this race!"

"I aim to do my best!"

Before they knew it, their tour was over and Lella was gone. Mira had known it would be a short visit. She was excited to be able to share the time with Xavier, who really was in childlike wonder. For as successful and worldly that he was, this experience seemed to be a highlight.

As they walked back to where they would meet the limo, Mira settled into an easy stroll.

"Lella is very kind to allow me to interlope into her time with you."

"You know as well as I do, there will not be much time visiting before the race ends."

"Si, they have a strict schedule. She calls you Mira, Mira."

Mira laughed. "Oh yes, she made it up to go along with the story of *Cinderella. Mirror, Mirror on the wall*, is the famous line."

"I like it Mira, Mira! Do you mind if I use it too? It's just too alluring."

"Not at all. It's a fun name. Much better than others that have been used in my lifetime."

"Care to share some of the others?"

"Absolutely not!"

"Aren't you being cryptic?" She could tell he was not offended.

"Not at all. I don't really like the others." She shrugged.

By that time, they had made it to the waiting car, and back to the condo they went.

****

"Where are we going to dinner?" Mira had walked out of her appointed bedroom, wearing what her mother labeled as, '*a girl's best friend—a little black dress.*' A black, pencil shaped dress, with a boat-neck and three-quarter sleeves. Elegant, yet understated. Simple black heels, and small purse.

"Wow, you look gorgeous!"

"Did I mention that I think you're a charmer?" She was feeling a little overwhelmed with his perusal of her from head to toe.

"I only speak truth. You are a very beautiful woman."

"Okay, enough with the compliments, please!"

"As you wish, for now anyway."

"So where are we going?"

"*Paris*. Dinner at the *Eiffel Tower*."

"Paris? That seems a little far from here."

"In Las Vegas, everything is nearby."

"Oh wait, you mean the *Paris, Paris Hotel*?"

"Si, we are having dinner at the *Eiffel Tower Restaurant*. French food."

"That sounds fancy. Am I underdressed for that?"

"What you have on is perfecto!"

"You look good in your suit; well put together." And he did look ready for the runway in his dark, charcoal grey suit, with matching shirt, opened at the collar.

"This is our dinner date. I needed to dress to impress!"

"Impress who?"

"Mira, Mira, you are adorable. Do you not get I am only interested in you? This is our first date, and it will be memorable."

"I didn't even think to ask about clothes to pack beyond race day gear, and the after party when Lella wins. My mother always says bring a black dress just in case."

"If there is something else you need or want, I will gladly supply it."

"I am practical. I am not shopping in expensive Las Vegas."

"What if you win a fortune at the casino?"

"I am not much of a gambler. And they say you have to play to win."

"Me either. I'd rather play games where the odds of winning are higher."

"Touché!"

"Shall we go?"

"Yes, I am ready."

They again met the driver who was at their disposal for the whole weekend. While the hotel was not very far, less than a mile, moving in Vegas during race week was difficult at best. Walking was not happening in heels, as Vegas blocks were long like those in New York City. Mira didn't care how long it took to get to the restaurant because being in Xavier's company was pleasant, fun and entertaining. Sometimes she found him challenging when he asked questions Mira felt were difficult to answer. Tonight though, was perfect. At least so far. She'd had enough time in his company to not be too nervous about their dinner.

They arrived at the main entrance, and doors were opened for them. A night on the town. Xavier escorted her through the hotel, and up to the eleventh floor of the replica of the famous Paris tower. Mira was sure she had never been to this restaurant before. It overlooked the strip and the *Bellagio's* fountains. The hostess showed them to a corner table surrounded by glass windows. Candles on the table, and an ice bucket, with a bottle. Once seated, the waiter appeared.

"Welcome to *Le Tour Eiffel*. Would you like champagne?" The waiter asked.

Xavier looked at her. "Querida, tonight is yours? Shall we have champagne?"

"Yes, that would be lovely." She said and a simple nod of deference.

They watched as the waiter made quick work of uncorking the bottle that had been chilled on ice. Pouring two glasses of the bubbly liquid, Mira actually was starting to feel like she was on a real date.

"Cheers to the woman who said yes to dinner with me, a date night!" He said lifting his glass.

She lifted her glass to meet his in a gentle clank.

"Miraculous, si?" She said with a challenge of her own.

"Magical just like I knew it would be." He said staring into her eyes.

Mira thought it a good moment take a sip.

"Ummmhmmmm. A good vintage."

"1989, a favorite year of mine."

"You surprise me!"

"Oh?"

"I'm impressed that you would even have tried a vintage from before you were born."

"You've done you research, Mira. I am simply sharing the finer things in life."

"I am very good at research."

"What do you want to know, that you couldn't find in your searches on me?"

Mira paused for a moment. That seemed like an open invitation. Would she take it? Hell yeah, she would.

"Why are you interested in me?" She asked setting her glass down.

"You make the days fun! As I mentioned before, you're smart, beautiful and creative. I'm attracted to you and I want to see where this goes." He seemed so sincere, so sure.

The waiter promptly reappeared to take their menu orders. They both chose salads, *Beef Wellington* for an entrée, and chocolate souffle for dessert. When the waiter disappeared, Xavier picked up where they left off.

"What else Mira? What are you afraid to ask me?"

Should she tell him, she paused again debating with herself.

"I want to know if you are using me as your next distraction?"

"I promise you, I am not."

"Okay. Thank you for answering my questions. Enough for one evening. I'd like to enjoy our dinner date, because this is where we are." She raised her glass once more towards him. "Cheers to a very good year, Xavier!"

"Cheers!'" He smiled with that devastatingly handsome glow in his eyes.

Throughout the meal, Mira felt more and more comfortable as she devoured the delicious food, and made small talk. She had to admit, she was attracted to Xavier's personality as much as she was to his candor, good looks and humor.

 "Thank you for a lovely meal, Xavier. I'm glad I came."

"The night is young…let's go up to the observation deck."

"I'd like that."

He escorted her up the elevator to the top of the replica *Eiffel Tower*, which stands forty-six stories above the city.

"This is said to be one of the most breathtaking views of Las Vegas." He noted as they stepped out onto the deck.

"There sure are a lot of lights here in the middle of a dessert." She laughed.

"Is the nickname of Vegas really '*Sin City*?'"

"Yes, a very prolific reputation for gambling, adult entertainment and all night adventures." Mira shivered with the cool breeze. She didn't have a jacket and the night temperatures were chilly.

"Are you cold?"

"Not really, just the breeze caught me off guard."

"Here, take my jacket." Xavier took his jacket and put it around her shoulders. She thought to resist, and then thought, why not. Its warmth enveloped her, and it had a faint scent of his alluring cologne.

They walked over to the railings. Mira mentioned the famous hotels, and pointed to where the Bellagio fountains were making beautiful music with the choreographed water works. In the opposite direction behind the hotel, they could see the *F1* symbol atop the race paddock area.

"We should get back to the condo. I don't want you to get sick!"

"I hate for the night to end." She said in almost a whisper.

"We still have race days." He reminded her.

"True. I have another question." Mira steeled her courage.

"Si, what is it?"

"Are you going to kiss me here on top of the world?" She said boldly.

"Is that your desire, Mira, Mira?"

"Yes."

"Then yes." He said and he gently pulled her into his arms. His lips touched hers in a tentative kiss. Mira sighed, and felt lost even as he held her against his firm body. It had been too long since she'd been properly kissed. All too soon their kiss ended. He stepped back from her, and the night air brought a chill once again. She shivered.

"Is something wrong?"

"Not at all. Dinner, a stunning view and our first kiss. I figured we better stop before you use it against me tomorrow."

"You think you can read me, huh?" She said in a saucy tone, placing her hand on her hip.

"No, querida. I'm just determined not to mess this up for either of us. I am caught up in this moment with you. We're staying in the same place, and we're not ready to go any further. Not yet."

"I'm sorry. You're right. Let's get back, and go to sleep. In separate bedrooms."

"I promise Mira that this is just the beginning for us."

Mira was so confused with his logic. Deep down she knew he was right. She would hate him by tomorrow if they slept together tonight. And she remembered she was here for Lella, not for frolicking in *Sin City*. Sobering as it was, there was no hurry for them to go any further. She would be satisfied with a great night in the perfect setting and with him. Tonight was magical…

Chapter 16

*"The winner ain't the one with the fastest car; it's the
one who refuses to lose."*
~ Dale Earnhardt

Practice Day One for *Formula One*, might seem like
any other Thursday for everyday folks in America.
However, it was the start of the three-day grand prix
spectacular that race enthusiasts and the who's who
rearranged life to attend. Xavier and Mira too, were
amongst those wanted to see the action. They went
back to the race zone a few hours early preceding the
first practice's start to meet Xavier's brother. Practice
one this year was set for six-thirty in the evening.
The plan was to get to just outside *The Sphere*
zone—the place they'd agreed to meet since so much
of the Strip was in lockdown. From there, they
would head over to the *Paddock* area, before the first
laps began. They had VIP passes so they weren't as
restricted as normal attendees. There would be
thousands descending into the spaces—everyone
ready to have a good time. There would be concerts,
interviews with race teams, and a festive good time.

The streets around the Strip had been cleared for the
race, and the bright street lights added to the
mystique of the brightest city on the planet even
before the sunset. Anyone wanting to move through
that zone either needed to be on foot, or be important
enough to have access where gates opened.
Occasionally, one might see a random golf cart
moving about. However, the street racetrack seemed
to be as undisturbed as possible awaiting time. Mira

had gotten lots of exercise walking around with Xavier earlier in the day. Now she was dressed in warm gear—fleece-lined pants, and a cashmere sweater just under Lella's circuit team jacket. That should be good enough to keep her warm. They had the luxury of going inside if it got too chilly. Xavier had on jeans and a matching race jacket to hers—both had received the gifts from Lella left for them at the condo.

When they arrived early to the VIP gate, Mira saw a few people standing around talking. She wondered if Xavier's brother was as early minded as he was. And then she spotted a man who looked to be a slightly older version of Xavier. No denying they were brothers, and of course he was an early bird too. Xavier must have spotted him as well, because he lifted his hand so the man would see him. They were close enough to the gate to pass the badge through to Matias. Once through security, he joined them. She watched the brothers hug briefly.

"Good to see you, Xa."

"Likewise." Xavier said stepping back and turning slightly. "Mira, let me introduce my brother, Matias."

"It is nice to meet you, Matias! You two look alike." Mira said smiling.

"Mira, the same here. I'm the more handsome brother. Xa doesn't introduce women to me, so I know you are special."

"Matias, really?" Xavier opened his arms in disgust.
"Mira, I am sorry about my brother's behavior."

"I am just speaking the truth." His brother said with
open arms, feigning innocence. Mira watched the two
and suppressed her laughter.

"Mira is special. I'm warning you! Don't scare her
off before we get to see this race. Because I will
pound you into the ground if you mess this up."
They all laughed together at that comment. Mira filed
away that statement wondering why Xavier didn't
bring women he was interested in around his only
sibling.

"I can already hear the banter between you two.
What a fun few days we are going to have!"

"Seriously, Mira, thank you for inviting me into your
circle. *Formula One* is a passion of mine. I was
never able to get our Papa to let me race. So instead,
I became an avid fan. Lella Rossi is about to
breakthrough on this circuit, and I am excited to be in
the entourage to celebrate the win!"

"I'm sure she will love that she has another fan! I'm
not so keen nor do I really understand this sport, so
I'm excited you and Xavier can drool together."

They all laughed again.

"Let's head over, so we are in place before they lock
down the zone."

And so it began…the practice days, test runs and qualifying went by in a blur for Mira. Except for the day they arrived, when Lella was able to meet them for a few minutes, she'd been off limits. From a distance, Mira could see her best friend and bask in the excitement of cars going at top speeds of two hundred plus miles per hour. It wasn't really Mira's forte, and both Xavier and Matias seemed to be enjoying themselves. They were speaking race lingo on many occasions and Mira tried to pick up details.

****

Race Night

On the final night of racing, the finale, they stood above the track in the suites area of the *Paddock Zone*. There were so many famous people in attendance, and Mira didn't care. She was only there to watch her friend excel at something she loved. Lella was in second place after the qualifying rounds. It all seemed to be going well, or according to plan, Mira surmised. After almost two hours of lots of back and forth position changes, it was a nail biter. Mira cheered and screamed along with the two Gutiérrez brothers. There was an easy-going familiarity they had with each other, and they had no problem bringing Mira in on their antics.

As Lella had predicted, she won! Mira hoped this was the beginning of many more winning races, and perhaps a circuit tour victory for Lella and her team. After the race, there were endless interviews, not just because she had won, but also because Lella was the first woman in modern history to win on the *F1* circuit. There was an outdoor fan fest and live music that would continue into the night for those who had witnessed the race. It was Vegas, so there were numerous after parties to last late into the night. Matias left them at the track and promised to come to the private *Mercedes* sponsored party, the one Lella had said she had to attend. Xavier and Mira had brought a change of clothes to the suite—and Mira's little black dress, freshly cleaned was her go to outfit. The night was young Mira knew, and with Xavier by her side she was content to enjoy all the sensory experiences.

****

After Party

"Ladies, if you'll excuse me for a few moments, I want to go see what the deejay has on his playlist." Xavier politely excused himself.

Mira and Lella nodded their heads in unison. She turned slightly to watch him walk away from their high-top bar table like a panther on the prowl. Damn he was so smooth, it added to his allure. She resisted the urge to sigh. Instead, she refocused on the drink in front of her. Twisting the little red straw around in her low ball glass, she wondered if perhaps another sip would calm her nerves. She certainly hoped so. She was not used to traveling with men. Or at least not this one. His smooth charisma had her off kilter and unsure of what to do next.

"Have you noticed the way he looks at you?" Lella said, interrupting her perusal.

"Excuse me?" She almost choked on the sip of gin and tonic that had just passed her lips. She leaned in closer to her friend.

"He's fallen for you, that one!" Lella pointed over her shoulder without turning around.

"Impossible! We literally just met a few weeks ago."

"I am not naïve, Mira. Not only has he followed you halfway around the world, he swoons with your every word. He's in love with you!"

"You've inhaled too many engine fumes, Lella! He might be curious to see if he can bed me, and perhaps he sees me as a challenge because he's used to getting what he wants. And lust is not the same as falling in love. I'm barely dealing with I'm here, with him."

"Oui, c'est vrai! You aren't dealing with it well." Mira ignored her friend's ability to switch from French and English all in the same sentence.

"Xavier has not fallen for me!" She said emphatically.

"She doth protest too much!" Lella said fanning herself in Shakespearean-style. "I'm looking forward to watching you two!

"Shut your mouth! Let this go and focus on winning the next damn race! Or let's celebrate tonight's win. That's why we're here, remember?"

"Cheers! To winning in many ways!" Lella held up her glass of tonic water with a sparkle of mischievousness in her eyes.

"Cheers!" Mira said begrudgingly. She knew her friend didn't much drink and definitely not while in race mode. Tonight would be it, and then she would get ready for the next race weekend.

"What are we cheering to?" She heard Xavier's voice from over her shoulder.

She turned slightly as he gracefully moved into the seat next to hers. She'd forgotten he'd gone off on his own mission.

"We, of course are cheering to Lella's success at the race." She lied, content to let the previous conversation die a quick death.

He held up his glass of whisky. "Here, here, cheers to the best *F1* racer ever, Lella! May you win big everywhere you go!"

All of them raised their glasses to that and she took a bigger gulp of her cocktail. As the liquid slid down her throat, she saw her friend wink at her. It was crystal clear! Lella was enjoying her squirming. Mira hoped it wasn't a mistake to have brought Xavier here. It seemed easy enough back in Florida for him to accompany her— just a few days of watching races. He'd gotten to see his brother, too. No harm, no foul. Or so she hoped.

"Of course you all are cheering the best race driver ever!"

"Everyone turned to see Xavier's brother, who must have just arrived at the party."

"Lella, this is my brother, Matias. He's your second biggest fan, behind me of course."

"I'm your first fan! Congrats Ms. Rossi. You were spectacular out there tonight."

"Oh, I love it…an entourage! Dedicated, flattering, loyal," Lella raised her glass. "It is nice to meet you Matias and thank you! And please call me Lella." Lella giggled as she offered her free hand in greetings.

Mira thought it best to speak up. "Lella, they really are your fans," she said shaking her head. "They definitely cheered louder than me at every session."

"Well, I am so excited to have won for my fans and my team! And now, I want to dance the night away!" She said setting her champagne glass down.

"Come dance with me?" Matias said offering his hand once more to Lella.

"Absolutely…" And just like that Matias and Lella disappeared into the crowded dance floor. Mira didn't expect that. And she didn't mind one bit having a few moments alone with Xavier.

"Do you want to dance the night away too, Mira?"

"Nope! I am happy just hanging out with you."

"Same here…I am the luckiest guy in the world."

Mira and Xavier chatted about the race while watching the dance floor. When Matias and Lella came back, they brought another woman with them.

"Mira, Xavier, I want to introduce you to my friend Becca. She flew in between assignments to watch the race as well."

"Nice to meet you, Becca."

"Same here," Becca said offering her friendly smile and handshakes all around. "I just wanted to come say hello. I have to get a plane back in a few hours. I have to be in Phoenix tomorrow morning."

"What do you do, Becca?"

"I own my own business. I'm a leadership coach and educator."

"Wow, that sounds amazing! We should talk when you have some time." Mira was definitely interested in getting to know this woman. She wondered if a leadership retreat for educators might make a difference. Teachers were an undervalued cornerstone of society.

"I'd love that. Lella can connect us after race season! A girls weekend. Perhaps we can stalk her race in Monte Carlo."

"Of course. Mi casa et su casa. Well thanks for coming to see me race Becca."

"Tata for now. I could stay here all night, and I would hate you all in the morning." Lella hugged the woman who seemed quite jovial. Becca waved goodbye to the rest of them before escaping into the crowded space.

"I think I'll be heading out too, Lella. You know I'm not the partying type. So I think I'm going to sneak away."

"Si, I am going to go with Mira!" Xavier said on the heels of her pronouncement. "I hope we get to see you race again soon!"

"The party is still booming though!" Lella gave a little pout on her face.

"You are still high on adrenaline, my dear. I'm crashing." It was after four in the morning and she was tired. Even though they were not leaving as early as Becca was today, Mira needed some sleep.

Lella giggled. "And full of champagne too, I'm sure."

"Well, I'm staying if that's okay with you, Lella?" Matias said holding his glass up. "The night is young!"

"Oh, there's at least one party animal to hang out with me!" Lella held up her glass, and Matias raised his as well.

"Suit yourself, Matias! And please do lookout for our famous friend!" Mira was glad that Matias was going to be around. Not that Mira was worried about her best friend. Security was tight and Lella was extremely responsible.

"Si, mi hermano, make sure Lella is safe!" Mira watched as a knowing look went between the two brothers. She was relieved, as Mira wasn't a fan of the fast lives and partying in Vegas.

They all hugged one another. Just as they were finishing up saying their goodbyes, Lella was asked to go meet with her race team for more celebratory toasts. That was Mira's signal to really go. They made their escape.

Chapter 17

"Life is short and we have never too much time for gladdening the hearts of those who are travelling the dark journey with us. Oh be swift to love, make haste to be kind."
~ Henri Frederic Amiel

"Wait you didn't sleep with him in Las Vegas?" Lella asked over the phone.

"No, that was our first date!" Mira exclaimed.

"And?"

"Not my thing." Mira reminded her friend.

"I get it, and weren't you tempted?"

"Of course I was, and I knew if I went in that direction, I would never allow him more of my attention."

"Yes, you can be quite decisive."

"You know, I was grateful you have such a spacious apartment. We each had our own space, and great breakfasts every morning on the balcony."

"I am so glad someone is getting use out of it. Other than the maid, of course. It seems like I am in that home so little of the time."

"Are you regretting being a racer? Being a winner? I mean it is a different lifestyle."

"Not at all. And I love sleeping in my own bed, walking barefoot on my own floor. I only have the two residences. While I am lucky to have both, I do not see them enough."

"Yes, for as much as I travel, there is no place like home."

"That's why we get along so well. You get what it's like to be a road warrior."

"Absolutely! I'm so glad we can confide in each other."

"Indeed. So are you going to sleep with him? Like, is it just a matter of time?"

"You don't hold back asking tough questions."

"Life is short. Might as well ask. What's your answer?"

"I think so. When the time is right."

"When's that gonna be?"

"Look, there's a race and theirs a circuit of races. I need to be sure this is more than a conquest. That I am more than a shiny toy he thinks he wants and can't have."

"True. Okay, keep me posted."

"I will. Now can we talk about your upcoming race?"

That was the end of the conversation about Xavier, thank goodness. Mira's call with Lella didn't last very long because Lella had to get back to her daily schedule. Mira admired the tenacity, discipline and grit it took for her friend to reach the top of her craft. For as exciting as it was to watch, she knew it was an exhausting schedule, not for the faint of heart.

****

Washington, DC

"Thanks again Mr. Godfrey." She shook the hand offered to her. The meeting had been intense and everything except an exact bloom date had been arranged.

"A pleasure Madam. We will closely watch the weather in the coming months. Just let me know if you need anything in the interim."

"Will do." She walked away from the smiling soul who had spent the last two hours poring through details. She paused just outside the ten foot doors of the lobby bar with their deep mahogany hues that towered above her. She felt short even in three-inch heels. *All in all, that went well.* She felt her phone vibrating in her hand. Looking down at the screen, she smiled. It was Xavier, who she hadn't yet assigned him his own ring tone. Too new, even if they had spent a long weekend together in Vegas. They'd parted on the promise of another date. so she wanted to take his call.

"Hi Mira, Mira! What are you up to?" He had taken on consistently calling her by Lella's nickname. It sounded extremely sexy in his thick Spanish accent.

"Hi yourself! I literally just stepped out of a planning meeting with the concierge at the *Omni Shoreham Hotel*. Might you hold for a brief few seconds?"

"Si. Of course."

"Thank you."

She moved across the lobby to one of the sitting areas that was unoccupied. She wanted to speak freely where she wouldn't immediately be overheard. Even as she thought that she knew the walls were always listening in this town. Placing her shoulder case on the table, she straightened her A-line skirt, and tucked it under her as she sat down in wingback chair of neutral tones. Exhaling, she put her headphones in and pressed the mute button to release the silence.

"I'm back!"

"Where are you?"

"Washington, DC."

"Wait, when did you go there?"

"This morning—quick two night trip."

"Oh I thought maybe you skipped town to avoid going on another date with me."

"While that's a funny idea, it's nothing like that. I had to rearrange my travel because of Lella's race. I am planning for the upcoming *Cherry Blossoms Festival* here in March. "

"I realized you'd be working, and yet I have no idea about Cherry Blossoms nor an *Omni Shoreham*. And what's a festival?"

"The *Cherry Blossom Festival*?

"Si. I have never heard of it."

"It's a month long festival that celebrates the gift of cherry trees from the country of Japan to the United States. They are planted around the *Tidal Basin* near the *Jefferson Memorial*. Every year, the trees flower in spectacular pinkish white blooms, and everyone celebrates! People from all over the country and the world flock to the city to take photos and be seen."

"What's the big deal?"

"I don't exactly know. They're beautiful. I went once. I think it has more to do with Spring coming, the religious holidays in which many are out of school and off work. They have outdoor events, parades, and so much more."

"Interesting! Do you have a specific event?"

"I have a group of ten women coming in for a bachelorette party. Only the best for their celebration they said. Wealthy folks have options. Theirs includes three possible weekend dates blocked because they want to be in town when the trees are in peak bloom. They want to take pictures and have a picnic. I am at the mercy of nature and it is quite stressful. So I need to make sure all the arrangements, limousines, party room, restaurants, bakeries, wines and entertainment are in process."

"I had no idea people could be so precise in their demands."

"Oh yeah, believe it! I used to be shocked by it. Now, I have adjusted."

"How were your requests received?"

"They were kind and gracious here. The conceding reminded me that this is why we selected the *Omni Shorem Hotel*. They are used to flexible plans, snobbery and the who's who because it's Washington DC."

"Tell me what you like most about the hotel?"

She sighed. He asked the most engaging questions. Rarely did anyone want her behind the scenes details, nor did they ask for her likes and dislikes.

"My favorite part of this hotel is the lobby? It's immense, yet charming, with beautiful crystal chandeliers, bright tones of off white, and mirrors. At the other end a large wide staircase that winds down twenty steps or so, with marble and plush carpet."

"Where do the steps lead?"

"Down to an open restaurant with a wall of windows that overlooks the gardens below the balconies."

"That sounds perfect for a women's event."

"Yes, I wanted to capitalize on the theme of a garden party. Many dignitaries marry off their children in these ballroom salons and gardens."

"Would you ever marry there?"

She paused. Such an intimate, odd question.

"I don't know if I would."

"Why not?"

"I never think about what my wedding will look like."

"Don't all women fantasize about their wedding day?"

"I don't." She said shifting uncomfortably in the leather wingback chair. "It's pretty enough, elegant, classy and perhaps a little too overwhelming for my tastes. I'm not into hundreds of guests or being seen."

"Understood. I just wanted to call so I could get on your calendar. When might that be possible?"

"Reach out to Miguel, and he will help you get onto my calendar."

"I definitely will do that. You know I miss you."

She paused, not wanting to say too much. "It is strange not being around you."

"I'll not put words into your mouth. And I think you're saying, you might miss me a little too?"

"Fine. Yes, I miss you too."

"That wasn't so hard to admit, no?"

"Hmmm. I will think more about that. In the meantime, I am sure you will consult Miguel, and he will let me know the date."

"Have safe travels, Mira, Mira."

"I will. Promise, and thanks for calling me."

They ended the call. As Mira sat in the beautiful lobby area, she watched couples come and go. She wondered what it might be like to be visiting Washington, DC with Xavier. When she'd wasted enough time, she arose from the chair, picked up her case and left all of it behind.

Chapter 18

"To us, family means putting your arms around each other and being there." ~ Barbara Bush

Xavier pulled up into the circle drive of Casa Gutiérrez, content to make a surprise appearance to see Tia Catherine, even though he was here to see TM. As he cut the engine of his *Mercedes* sedan, he exhaled. He loved being home, yet he was not thrilled by the reason. He approached the large brown double doors that sat below the entry portico, and reached for the metal handle. First thought was always to check the door, not ring the bell or knock. Sure enough when he put his hand on the metal handle and pressed it down, it gave way, opening with a chime to let anyone who might be in the front rooms know that somebody was coming in. This door was typically unlocked, especially before the wee hours of the early morning. Someone was always awake, and the security of the estate had cameras strategically hidden to observe the comings and goings. The extra surveillance was not to invade the sense of privacy of its occupants, family members or workers. More so, it was meant to keep the wrong crowd out—the paparazzi, and those who might seek to do some harm. While there was a main gate that was monitored, there were lots of opportunities for people to trek in on foot and be unnoticed until caught by security in the wrong place.

Walking into the entryway, Xavier closed the door quietly. The living room was off to the left, first doorway and it was the center of their family life. To make a proper entrance, he best go see if anyone was there. He turned the doorknob and peeked in. There he saw his Aunt and Uncle lounging on the couch. Tia was reading a book with her feet on Tio Antonio's lap as he read the newspaper. They led such a simple life, even though the family's olive oil business was a global brand. All the comforts of home and love were on display in this Spanish palace. Perhaps that was why it was home—a safe space for all of them to gather.

"Buenos tardes Tio, Tia!"

"Xavier, back so soon?" His aunt said looking up from her book.

"Tia, I'm hurt. Are you not happy to see me?" He said as he came into the room.

"Si, of course. I just find it strange that you are here more often than not when Tomas is home. Is that a coincidence?" Xavier gave his Tia a quick kiss on both cheeks. Tio nodded. He didn't want to disrupt their cozy scene.

"I actually did come to check on him. Being in trouble with you and Tio is never good."

"I wish you would impart that wisdom to my wayward son. It has been most difficult to get him to settle down."

"I'm sure he will in time, Tia."

"How about you? When are you going to settle down? Take a wife, have some children that I can spoil?"

"Catherine, give the man a reprieve. He's come to counsel that child you spoiled too much." Tio Antonio spoke up to his wife.

"Really Antonio! This is not my fault. All I've ever wanted is for my sons and nephews to meet nice women, marry and make babies."

"You are a control freak, my love!"

"I am not!" His aunt said in a terse voice.

Xavier was grateful to his uncle for the distraction, and took that as his cue to escape.

"Great seeing you two. I'll stop back before I go," Xavier said as he departed the living room.

"Please do," Tia said not turning her attention from her husband. "Now husband, try to say nice things to me or else…"

Xavier closed the door not wanting to hear any more of the spat between his favorite couple. He had enough to worry about, and he had no desire to endure yet another shaming by his Tia for not settling down yet.

He'd check in on his cousin, and then leave the Palazzo before lunch was served, thereby escaping

being questioned again. He wanted to call Mira and
check on her anyway. Today was the American
holiday of Thanksgiving. She'd said she was going
to her parents, even though she didn't really want to.
He called Mira every day for no other reason than to
hear her voice, laughter and to remind her he hadn't
forgotten that they'd have another date. He wasn't
due back to Florida until the first week in December.
He took the steps, two at a time. That was always the
fun of growing taller when they were younger. At
the top, off to the right he went to his cousin's room.
He had gambled that TM would be there hatching a
plot to sway his parents to let him escape. The in-
and-out of trouble routine had been going on for
years. He knocked on the door.

"Come in," he heard his cousin from the other side of
the door.

Turning the doorknob, Xavier opened the door to see
his cousin sitting in a wingback chair, watching
television. Remote in one hand and cell phone in the
other.

"Hey Xa! What's up? Didn't know you were back."

"I'm not. It's an illusion of your imagination." He
didn't move further into the room.

"Oh you have jokes! Well some of us are trapped
here, and can't escape. Are you going to sit?"

"You brought that on yourself. I told you not to go to that party without me." Xavier moved across the room to sit in the swivel chair behind the desk.

"How could I turn down a Princess?" His cousin shrugged, not turning from the tv.

Xavier rolled his eyes. "I've heard that way too many times. How about you learn to say no?"

"Come on Cuz, you know how it is? The parents taught us that we have to put on a unified front, be an olive branch of goodwill."

"Oh please! You're talking to me, remember? I am not persuaded by that crap you tell your parents. I wish you would listen to me."

"Et tu, Brutus! Did they send you to talk to me?"

"They did not. I came of my own free will. I must say Tia did mention what I am already sure she has observed—I come when you've gotten into trouble. If we're not careful, she might start to think I am the reason you keep getting in trouble. I would really be angry at you if that happens."

"I doubt that she'd ever think that. You're too much of a goody two shoes. Mama indulges me, and she knows I mean no harm. I like having fun. Trouble just seems to follow me!"

"I don't have the luxury of being spoiled like you. I have to work. I like working. Taking care of myself, making my own money and being responsible—it keeps me under the radar.”

“Is that meant to sway me? Boring!”

Xavier threw a pen across the space trying to hit his cousin. TM caught it before it landed.

“I do appreciate you. Always we’ve remained close. I can talk to you about stuff I can’t tell my other brothers. You get me. They just like to lecture me.”

“Well just be aware, my patience does have its limits.”

“I know. I’m thinking about how I can do better. I am going to turn over a new leaf.”

“What are you talking about? You? You’re done being the rich playboy, out for a good time?”

“I’m working on myself. I’m going to start afresh with the new year. Right after all the holiday parties.”

Xavier put his head in his hands, and shook it slowly.

“Really, I’m serious!”

“Okay, let’s just say you’re on the right track. You wouldn’t just be saying that so you can get out of this prison sentence?”

"Absolutely not! I just need a few more weeks of fun, and then with the new year, I am going to be a new man."

"This, I can't wait to see! Have you told tus padres?"

"Nope. I am going to show them."

"I hope it works."

"It will, trust me. I'm good. Wanna go get some drinks in town and watch the futbol match?"

"Oh no! You are not using me to get out of the house. You have to serve your penance without me being your advocate with Tia!"

"Fine! I'll watch it here on the big screen downstairs. You gonna stay?"

"No, I have to go. I have some calls to make. I really just wanted to stop through for a quick visit."

"Thanks for coming to check on me!"

"That's what cousins are for!" He got up from the desk and went to the center of the room to give his cousin a hug goodbye. Quick hug, and he escaped into the hallway. He really did hope this time TM was heading in the right direction, permanently. Xavier wasn't convinced and he knew only time would tell.

****

"Hey you," she said stretching her legs from under her as she laid across her bed.

"Hola Mira, Mira. How is Thanksgiving going?"

Mira sighed. "It was bearable, My parents had all the usual foods. My mother had most of it prepared for us, and my dad happily watched football. My grandma kept me company for most of it, until she fell asleep in the rocking chair. I just got home about thirty minutes ago."

"That sounds festive!"

"That's a nice way to say 'boring.'"

"You have a mother and grandmother. Boring is good."

"Yeah, I suppose you're right!"

"What did you eat?"

"Mashed potatoes, turkey, and apple pie."

"Those are interesting choices."

"They're my favorite foods. And they're a guarantee at our house."

"I'll remember that in the future."

"You don't have to. I don't often eat my favorite foods."

"Why not?"

"It's not good to indulge too much in the things one really wants."

"Where did you learn that?"

"I'm not sure. Can we change the subject though?"

"Of course, querida."

"What have you been up to in Spain?"

"I've been visiting my cousins, and their parents, Tio Antonio and Tia Catherine. And of course working."

"No soccer or wild parties."

"No. My cousin Tomas behaves when he is summoned home. He tried to get me to go out and I thought it best to decline."

"Your cousin sounds like a handful."

"Si, well that's been said before. I think he's been spoiled for too long and just needs to grow up!"

"Perhaps you are being a better influence on him than he is on you."

Xavier laughed heartily. "Perhaps! We are hopeful. Tia and Tio are losing their patience."

"Are you losing your patience with him too?"

"Not really. It's hard being the youngest. Especially in our family of mostly male children."

"You're the youngest, and you don't seem to get into as much trouble as your cousin."

"I don't like publicity. Tomas seems to crave it."

"I see."

"Enough about that. I miss you."

She smiled. "I miss you too. When are you coming back to Florida?"

"Why? Are you ready for another date?"

"Perhaps," she said using his non-committed tact.

"I'll be back December 1st. Can I come by the office and see you?"

"Yes."

"Great. Talking to you has been wonderful. And it doesn't take the place of being in your space."

"I already said yes! Don't make me blush…"

"I'm just telling you my truth. Plus, I like that I have the power to make you blush."

"Don't get too carried away."

"I won't. What are you doing with your weekend?"

"Working. How about you?"

"Working too."

"We are a fun bunch!"

"I promise we'll do something fun, when I get back to Florida."

"Very cool. Thanks for cheering me up."

"A pleasure. Sweet dreams, querida."

"You too." She clicked off the phone happy that he'd called. Maybe there was more to life than endless working and obligatory holidays with family. For tonight though, she was tucked in and happy it had been an uneventful day. She would sleep well and perhaps dream about Xavier…

Chapter 19

*"Once you have commitment, you need the discipline
and hard work to get you there."*
~ Haile Gebrselassie

Xavier had come into Mira's office. She motioned for
him to take a seat, and held up five fingers so as not
to interrupt her call. She was wrapping up the
Oleander honeymoon details with the resort's general
manager, Gustavo, who was on speakerphone. The
client, a shipping magnate marrying a Greek heiress.
As such, she expected over the top requirements and
results. Just the location itself was spectacular. The
Maldives— the most desired honeymoon on the
planet. They'd opted for a resort where they could
interact with other people over renting a private
island. She would make sure it was unforgettable.

"And where do I send the custom beach towels?"

"How will they be coming?"

"By *FedEx*."

"Then send them under my name to the *Full Moon
Resort*."

"Okay very good." She jotted down her checkmark
near the bottom of the list of items to finalize.

"When will they show up?"

"They will arrive seven days before and will have
Mr. and Mrs. embroidered on them. There will be a
set of seven. Seven is a good luck number. They will
need to be washed throughout the week. Do you have
the ability to do that?"

"Of course, it will be arranged." Gustavo had given
into her every request so far.

"Excellent. At the end of their stay, please wash
them. I will bring the label to ship home upon my
arrival for set up. It's possible they might want to
take one or two with them."

"Very good. I will make note and see to it myself."

"Thank you. This is why I recommend your resort
because of the stellar service."

"It is our pleasure."

"At the end of their stay, my client will be surprising
his bride with a new yacht that was commissioned for
them."

"What is the boat name so we can be on the
lookout?" He didn't seem phased one bit by the
luxurious gift.

"Hold on. Let me check the notes." She sorted
through some of the papers. Her staff had captured
more of the details for her after the initial client
meeting.

"Here it is. It's the *Cinnamon Spice*."

"That sounds intriguing."

"It does, right?"

"Any other details?"

"The yacht will arrive in your marina the day before their departure. There will be a chef and staff on board. I asked if they needed any provisions from the resort, and was told no."

"Very good. I will advise the marina captain."

"I think that's all for now. I will arrive three days prior and stay through their first night, as discussed. Thank you again Gustavo. I appreciate all of your efforts and those of the resort. The groom is spending a fortune to impress his bride."

"Understood and we shall not disappoint!"

"I will look forward to seeing you again. Ciao for now."

Xavier wasn't trying to eavesdrop, and yet how could he not with the call on speakerphone. Mira seemed quite chummy with this Gustavo guy. He didn't like it and he forced himself to let it go. She was conducting business and was acting the consummate professional. He was not worried, per se. He outshined all competition when he set his mind to having his heart's desires. And Mira was worth all the effort. He'd figure out how to keep her attention or die trying.

She clicked the button on the phone.

"Sorry to have been rude. We are getting close to the date for this one. Plans are almost set so I want to make sure we're ready."

"Where is the *Full Moon Resort* in the world? Clearly somewhere with some water if there is a yacht involved."

"The Maldives."

"Wow!"

"Ever been there?"

"No, and I've heard its beautiful with crystal clear water."

"Yes, it is."

"Perhaps one day, I will go there."

"You're welcome to come with me if you have the time. It's to be in a little under two weeks from now."

"I'd love to go anywhere with you."

"Anywhere?"

"Si. And in all seriousness, let me check my calendar and get back to you. I'll pay my own way.

"No need. Business expense. If it works into your schedule, let Miguel know and he'll make the arrangements."

"Now, how about dinner tonight?"

"Oh that sounds lovely." Mira's phone rang. She put up her fingers again to gesture for five minutes.

"Mira here."

Xavier flipped through the portfolio of travel adventures that was laying on the desk. Mira seems to be arranging some adventure that included painting. The call only lasted four minutes.

"Not to eavesdrop, and what's a sip and paint retreat?"

"It's like a creative relaxation weekend. The client wants to spend three days with her friends being creative, relaxing and having fun."

"Did they come up with that idea?"

"Nope, I did."

"You really do think outside the box!"

"Remember the questionnaire I had you complete?"

"Si."

"It gives me ideas to pitch to the client. I go with their lead, and ultimately they choose."

"I bet they think it is their idea."

"Sometimes, and I don't mind. A lot of my success comes from delivering the adventure, not solely from the ideas."

"I agree. At least that's what my cousin noted too."

"So, where would you like to have dinner?"

"It doesn't matter. You choose. I get tired of making decisions all day. It will be nice to just go and enjoy."

"I'll arrange something. It might not be as extravagant as the *Eiffel Tower*."

"I don't need extravagant. Chinese carryout works. Anything is good as long as it's with you!"

Chapter 20

"No one is as deaf as the man who will not listen."
~ Proverb

Later that week...

"Hi Mira. I got your message." Lella said.

"How are you? I wasn't going to leave a message. Your agent insisted."

"Yes, I pay him a lot of money to take messages. He said your friend called. When I asked which friend, he could never tell me who. I figured I would start with you."

"You could get a messaging service."

"Who are we kidding? Then I would never return anyone's calls. I need prodding, especially during the season."

"I hate bothering you." Mira begrudgingly said.

"Mira Morales, what's going on? What aren't you telling me?"

"You know I'm low key. I don't like drama!"

"I do. What drama could you possibly have caused?"

"Not me. I just saw this article on Xavier. It seems to be about him and his cousin being the life of the party—wild nights with wild women." Mira didn't mention the exact contents that bothered her the most—with one woman.

"Who says what your reading is true?"

"I don't know."

"Did you ask him?"

"No."

"Why not?"

"I don't want him to think I'm bothered!"

"But you are bothered, Mira."

"Ugh! I know!"

"Look I'm not one to offer advice. And I'm going to say, as someone the paparazzi chase, it's hard not to be misconstrued and innocent moments are often taken out of context."

"You are not like him! He's a playboy!"

"Does he act like a playboy around you?"

"No and he is charming! Even my assistant can't function when he calls or stops by."

"Mira, stop the madness! Trust me when I say, he is the only one who can tell you the truth."

"I know you're right. Can we change the subject?"

"Of course!"

"How are you? Any new news about you?"

"Nothing really new. Same old stuff…practice, travel and racing."

"You live a great life, Lella!"

"I do. And sometimes I want quiet time, anonymity."

"You'd be so bored!"

"I would not. I would go to the market, come home, cook a meal and eat on my balcony."

"You would not. I remember my client checklist. You hate cooking."

"Well maybe because I don't practice it."

"You practice not, because you want not!"

They both burst into laughter.

"You got me Mira! Perhaps after the season, I'll take a cooking class."

"Yeah, just let me know if you want me to arrange something. I have some contacts in that industry. They'd love to take you on!"

"I forgot your contact list extraordinaire. I'll let you know!"

"Ha, I get it. Don't call me, I'll call you!"

"Well anyway. Remember my advice. I gotta get to the track."

"I will, I promise!"

Mira would take her best friend's advice. Being anxious wasn't helping. The best advice was to ask the source. At some point, perhaps she would ask Xavier to explain. In the meantime, she needed to put her focus on other things, like work.

Chapter 21

"Romance is the glamour which turns the dust of everyday life into a golden haze."
~ Elinor Glyn

Two Weeks Later

"Welcome to your villa—your home away from home for the next four nights!"

"Thank you," they both said in unison as the bell captain showed them into their two-bedroom accommodations at the *Full Moon Resort* on its own island near Male, Maldives. Then he left them with his promise to bring the luggage.

As she had offered, Mira had brought Xavier along on her pre-trip before her clients arrived in three days. She purposefully chose a two-bedroom villa as she wasn't trying to make promises she couldn't keep. She'd know if the right time came to take their relationship to another level, and she still wasn't ready.

The villa had every amenity—separate bedrooms with king sized beds, a private pool that sat on a lanai across from and accessible to each room, with a tree-lined path walkout to the beach. After checking out the space, Mira was standing in the common area looking out the patio doors at the pool.

"Is your room acceptable?" She asked turning to face Xavier when she heard footsteps. She figured he wouldn't be as picky as many of her clients so she hadn't bothered to ask for his travel requirements.

"It's very posh, si?" He stood on the other side of the living room behind the couch, and closest to his bedroom.

"You do understand separate bedrooms?" She said hoping he would.

"Mira, of course. I am here to watch you in action, working your magic. Perhaps a little of your attention in paradise if you have time—a dinner or sun bathing on the beach. I don't expect anything more."

"Thank you for giving me some space to deal with our attraction!"

"Oh, I know I'm very attracted with you. And I have patience. All in good time. You will not be giving into me. You will be giving into yourself!"

"Thanks!" Mira knew he was right. She was in a debate with herself to be sure, to know for sure what she could depend upon. He said nothing more, and yet it felt that he could see right into her indecision. She needed to break this silence. At least this time. *Say something safe…*

"The only thing I haven't seen is the restroom."

"Let me show you! It's outside." Xavier said, as walked back towards the main entry door at the front of the one level villa. She followed close behind and as he stopped, she watched him open a door on the right side of the wall.

If Mira had not been following closely behind him, she would have sworn she misheard him say, "it's outside." Through the brown wooden door, he stepped down into an outside oasis, and she too entered the enclosed outdoor space. On the immediate left, there was a white bowl sink and mirror above. In front of her was a separate wooden stall for the toilet with a frosted glass door. And a marble stone tile pathway that lead to an open air shower, with blue skies overhead. There was also a large jacuzzi type bathtub. Surrounding the pathway was a garden of natural flora and fauna, and it was all encircled by ten foot stone walls.

"Wow, am I dreaming this? I know I'm tired after the long flights, and this is unexpected!" It took a lot to impress her, and this outdoor oasis was breathtaking! She walked further into the garden setting, and immediately felt the heat of the sun beat down on her.

"It's definitely not an illusion," he said coming to stand in the open courtyard next to her.

"Look at the waterfall nozzle up there. Is it going to feel like a rain shower? What if it rains? Kind of defeats the purpose, huh?"

"Just add soap and rinse off!" He said jokingly.

"Ha-ha funny!"

"I do think this is the most beautiful shower I have ever seen."

"Me too," she said looking on the ground at the species of indigenous plants. She moved her head, watching closely.

"What exactly are you looking for? Did you drop something?"

"No, I just saw a little lizard eat a flower and escape into the bushes. It was so fast."

"No way!"

"I am not crazy, I saw it!"

"Are you afraid of lizards?"

"No, as long as they stay in their own space, not mine."

"All of this, is their space," she watched as he waved his hands across the garden.

"I'm much happier with the saying, '*out of sight, out of mind*!'"

"This saying, I am not familiar with it."

"It means if I can't see it, then I can pretend it's not here and be happy."

"Well Mira, Mira, just call me and I will come to your rescue!"

"What if I don't have any clothes on?"

"I will be fully dedicated to the task at hand and will not be distracted by your naked beauty."

"Yeah right!"

"I swear," he said making the sign of the cross over his heart. "Just make sure to leave the door unlocked so I don't have to scale the walls."

"Oh now you're making fun of me."

"Not at all querida," he said pulling her into his arms. He brushed a curl behind her ears. "I promise to watch over you!" His lips found hers and she no longer cared about the possibility of showering with lizards.

Their kiss ended so fast, leaving her longing for more.

"Sorry Mira. I couldn't resist." He said stepping back from her.

"It's okay. It was actually a very nice kiss."

"I'm not sure anyone has ever said that to me before."

"I suspect you are also not used to traveling with a woman that you are not sleeping with either."

"Sleeping with? You probably are not being literal, right?"

Mira just shook her head. "You are definitely being a jokester! We're tired. How about we change into beachwear, find some food, and get acclimated to paradise?"

"That sounds like a great idea!"

Mira sighed as he stepped aside to let her walk back into the cooled, interior room. She hoped she wouldn't be swayed in this romantic paradise by the charms of this man. She had work to do. Plus, it was too soon to be getting carried away, no matter how sexy he was staring at her like a flower to the lizard, in these surroundings a world away from the safe boundaries of home.

****

"So do you like it here?"

She spun around from lying on her stomach, reading a paperback. "What's not to like? I am getting paid to sample the beach, looking out over water that is clear to the bottom, and soaking up the sun. I don't have to worry about hurricanes or typhoons. This is paradise on Earth!"

"No, I mean do you like how remote it is here?

"Oh that. We're only here for a few days. I like the quiet of this moment!"

182

He watched as she dropped the book, moving herself to a seated position on the lounger. Oddly, she lowered her glasses, looking across the water as if something important were happening across the bay. He wondered if she was soaking in the stillness of the scene. He wanted to follow the direction of her intent. Yet with nothing hiding her eyes, he was captivated and could not look away. Already her sun-kissed skin radiated warmth in the hour they'd been on the beach. And the two-piece mocha bikini that hid little from his imagination was setting his libido on fire. He doubted an ice bath could temper his newly discovered insatiable desire for her. *Rein in your thoughts man!* He knew logically, this, them, was in its infancy and at times she seemed like she'd run for the hills. No question. He wanted her. He longed to be inside her branding her to him. All in due time, he hoped she'd acquiesce to the growing passion between them and act on her desires. He heard her voice, and refocused.

"And in a few hours a lot of this solitude is going to be taken up with the making of arrangements, having meetings with the chefs, setting up for the clients, and planning for the next client. It doesn't seem like I will be bored. What about you?"

"I definitely like sitting here on the beach with you. I can't remember the last time I sat on a remote beach."

"Oh right. You're more used to partying on the back of yachts in the south of France!"

"Ouch! You've seen those photos, have you?"

"Well let's just say it's hard to miss you and your cousins living *La Vida Loca*."

"I think I mentioned before, my cousin, Tomas, and my brother are the party types. Not the rest of us. I was sent to be the voice of logic as I have been told on numerous occasions. Also, someone needs to be around to clean up their messes."

"How noble of you!"

He laughed half-heartedly and the humor didn't reach his eyes. Rarely did he complain and yet with Mira, he wanted to be honest.

"Seriously, I hate that lifestyle! I work hard for our family business, and managing our reputation is part of the territory. I don't have to like it to be effective."

"You didn't look miserable dancing the night away nor toasting as the champagne flowed."

"Si, I suppose it might seem that way. As I said before, I recommend you not believe everything you see and read."

"Let me recall the caption." She paused. He knew she was going to bring it verbatim to their blissful solace. So be it.

She turned her head, to look him in the eye. "*Will he or won't he settle down? Xavier Gutierrez has been seen on more than one occasion with mystery woman. Sources close to the playboy say he's about to pop the question.*"

"Mira, I am not in a relationship nor am I a playboy. End of story, or in this case, end of tabloid lies."

He'd said there was nothing to those tabloid stories. Who would admit to being caught red-handed, especially if it stood in the way of them getting what they wanted? That was just being human. She did want to believe him.

He knew every word of the article and the furthest thing from his mind was to discuss Dana. Even Tia Catherine had chastised him for being careless in who he took up with; she begged him to stop seeing Dana even though he'd explained it was harmless flirtatiousness. Weeks ago, the Italian woman had ended their tryst. It had worked out and he didn't protest beyond mild interest about Dana's motive. Had Tia pulled some strings or bribed the woman to break it off. He didn't care. That was right before he met Mira, and now she consumed his interest. Perhaps he was ready to leave casual behind. There was definitely something unique about Mira's bold, straight-talk personality, coupled with her ability to hear what wasn't being said. Her mannerisms suggested she was a '*take no prisoners*' kind of person. That suited him just fine as he suspected she'd always let him know where he stood, even if he didn't like it. Too many people brooded without getting the answers they needed.

"What happened to the last one?" He could see her squinting with the bright sunshine as her eyes tried to adjust.

"The last what?" He smiled, amused by her question.

"The last woman you were interested in?" And she appeared not to be backing down on the subject either.

"She found someone to love, and walked away."

"I'm sorry Xavier." Wow, she actually said that with compassion. Another trait he filed away.

"Don't be. It wasn't serious!" He sort of hoped she'd be a little bit jealous and declare she was glad Dana had moved on.

"So now you need a new distraction. Me? Until someone else catches your eye?"

"Mira, Mira on the wall?" He lowered his glasses and stared into her warm brown eyes. "There is no one else who distracts me from you!"

"For now, perhaps."

"We're the only two on this beach. Do you deny it? Am I distracted?" There was no distraction. He

ignored her attempt to goad him. and he paused,
waiting for her next move.

"Touché, Xavier!"

"Excelente." He pushed his dark glasses back into
place to again shade his eyes.

She sighed as she looked out into the sun-drenched
ocean. The water was so crystal-clear and yet it
shimmered with blue-green hues that made one
wonder where the magnificent colors emerged. If
only she were clear about this situation. Or non-
situation as Xavier had reminded her. It was just the
two of them, here alone and undisturbed in this
idyllic setting.

"It sizzles here with the sun between us. Come swim
with me?" He said.

She watched as, like a gazelle, he lifted himself off
the beach chair, and held a hand out for her. She was
about to say no, and then she thought better of it. A
harmless swim in paradise.

"Why not?" she said.

Xavier wasn't sure she would say yes to his
invitation. And she had. He'd take the small win that
she agreed to a swim. He watched as she pushed her
sunglasses back into place to shield herself from him
once more. He felt the shift. They were now
separated like a force field—a wall she erected to
keep him at arm's length. For him, she was like

whipped butter on a hot roll. Confident, sexy and smooth. They were the only two people around. No paparazzi, no other beach goers, no place they had to be—just the two of them on this desolate beach in the middle of nowhere. He loved her job. Work hard, play hard! And he was definitely committed to take advantage of some fun in the sun with Mira…

****

Later that evening…

"You ready?"

Mira walked into the common area wearing a simple elegant blue maxi dress. He looked up from the magazine he'd been staring at or more like imagining her in all stages of undress. It had been quite unproductive and he had no memory of what was contained in the pages of the guide to the Maldives. After being on the beach, frolicking in the water with her, and a refreshing shower, he was ready for a quiet evening where they could just relax. Soon enough, they'd go back to the chaos of life in the real world.

"Si. Ready, if you are!" He stood up.

"Our reservation is in a few minutes. I couldn't decide what to wear."

"You look amazing. Blue is stunning on you."

188

"I wasn't fishing for compliments. I'm just not sure what the night air will hold, and I want to be prepared so I do not have to be uncomfortable."

They were having dinner at the resort's *Sea Salt Restaurant*. There were multiple choices of where to eat. Mira had simplified it—there or Thai, she'd asked. They opted for the candlelight restaurant. Well actually, he had chosen. Mira had asked him to choose from a male's point of view. Research she called it. He liked the idea of the al fresco setting with candlelight by the sea.

"Might I recommend you bring a wrap for your shoulders, just in case?"

"Great idea. Let me get it."

He was rewarded by his great idea in seeing her turn, and the silhouette of the dress giving way to more of her figure. He wanted her so much. And nothing about his desire would have him move too fast. This was a delicate operation. Moments later when she had returned, he moved to the wooden door that would lead them out front and onto the sandy path that winded through the resort and led to the main area of life. He held it open for her to precede him, and he caught the faint whiff of jasmine and vanilla as she walked by. It was so intoxicating he briefly closed his eyes as he inhaled, and stepped outside into the humid night. He had on tan khaki slacks, a matching polo shirt, and already he was starting to sweat.

"It's not too bad out here. Definitely, I knew it was still warm because the shower is outside."

Her comment broke the spell. "Si, I wasn't sure what would happen after sunset, and it definitely is still quite warm."

"At least there is a faint breeze."

"And ice water, I hope at the restaurant!"

She laughed. "We'll soon find out."

The restaurant was the distance of a short city block away from their villa. The path was wide enough to accommodate the occasional golf cart, which was the main mode of transportation on the small island. He reached out to put his hand casually on her lower back as they strolled along. There was nothing else that needed to be said. Companionable silence was nice with a woman. He appreciated that she didn't need to fill every moment with lots of chatter like many women he'd been around. You could get to know people in other ways than just by talking.

"Reservation for Morales," he heard Mira say as they approached the front of the outdoor restaurant.

"Would you prefer inside or out?"

Mira looked over to him. "Preference?"

"Is by the water available?"

"Yes, sir. We are not forecasted to have any rain showers tonight. The evening will be very pleasant."

The hostess walked them across the restaurant that was shaped like an open-air circle, littered with intimately set tables, adorned with white cloths, fine china, glassware and shimmering lit candles. Under their feet, tightly packed sand that didn't give way under the weight of their walking. Xavier thought this to be the perfect setting for Mira to be reminded there was more to life with him than just work. He'd cleared his schedule, and told his staff not to interrupt his trip unless it was an emergency with Papa. They would have an easy-going, relaxing evening.

He seated her and then took his place in a chair across the linen-covered table. When the waiter arrived with the wine list, all he could think was champagne. So he ordered a bottle. After it was delivered, glasses poured, and the remainder put on ice, he lifted his glass.

"Mira, Mira, cheers to a great night! Bon Santé!"

He watched as she lifted her glass, with a smile and tilt of her head, she too said, "Cheers!"

Dinner was delicious, and their night ended on a stroll back to the villa. Just inside the door, Xavier paused.

"Mira, thank you for a lovely evening. Buenos noches!" He bowed slightly, kissed her on both cheeks, and went to his bedroom.

"Goodnight, Xavier." Was all he heard her say as he walked away. It took all his resolve to walk away from her without even a proper kiss goodnight. And he needed to let her be sure.

The rest of the trip in the Maldives was quite busy. He watched Mira in her element making sure everything was in place for the honeymooning couple. Xavier was actually able to get some design work done. He attributed his creativity to the scenery and the inspiring woman who was like the *Energizer Bunny*, with boundless energy.

Chapter 22

"In family life, love is the oil that eases friction, the cement that binds closer together, and the music that brings harmony." ~ Friedrich Nietzche

Days Later

Ponte Vedra, FL

"Good Morning, Dad!"

"Good Morning, Scoot! " She watched as her dad set aside his newspaper. The club made sure that there was "new" news in the early hours before most of the members went to golf tee times or tennis lessons.

"Where's mom?" She said leaning over to kiss the top of her dad's head before dropping her keys on the table and taking her seat across from him.

"She wasn't feeling great this morning?"

"Is she alright? We could have canceled." Mira said, concerned.

"Mira, you have canceled the last three Sundays. So your mother thought it best I come find out what's going on with you!"

Mira was suddenly on alert. "So she sent the good cop. I see!"

"No. I'm not doing your mother's bidding. I too, am curious to set my eyes upon you. Make sure you're okay."

"Dad, I call every day. Don't you think I would tell you if there was anything wrong?"

"I didn't say there was anything wrong. Place your order and have some coffee before you tell me what has you so distracted." He motioned for the server to come. It was their routine to get the greetings out of the way before they placed their order. '*The walls have ears*,' her mom would say. Mira didn't much care who overheard whatever she was saying. Yet, her parents abhorred gossip, especially about them.

Mira wanted a simple breakfast today, anyway. She had gone for a walk on the beach at dawn to clear her mind. Her parents' instincts were spot on. She was distracted by one, Xavier Gutiérrez, and how attracted she was to him. She would not confess it that way though.

"Good day Ms. Mira. What will you have today? Coffee?" The server, Ms. Emma, had been at the club for as long as Mira could remember.

"Good day back to you, Ms. Emma! Yes, coffee and lite fare today please. Dry wheat toast and a banana." Mira watched the coffee get poured into the white mug that magically had appeared in front of her.

"Coming right up, with dry wheat toast and a banana for the young miss. Mr. Morales, I will bring more coffee."

"Thank you," they both said in unison.

"Always a pleasure." Just like that, and Ms. Emma was gone.

"As I was saying, your mother and I want to hear what's got you so distracted." It was a statement, not a request.

"I have a lot going on with work, that's all."

"Don't insult my intelligence, my dear. I know you. Your work is always demanding, and you thrive on staying busy. Yet, you aren't distracted for weeks on end like you've been these last ones. You're grown. I would rather you simply say: *Butt out, Dad*!"

"It's not that. I met someone through work. And it's complicated."

"How so? Are they threatening you? Stalking you? We can call Detective Darryl at the department."

"Oh no, it's nothing like that. I like him. Far too much and too soon!"

"Oh, I see. You've met someone who just might be worth your time and effort?"

"Yeah, something like that." She watched her dad lean forward in his chair. Lecture time. She held her breath for the wisdom about to come, whether she wanted it or not.

"Life's an adventure Mira. I know I don't have to tell you that. And it seems like you need to hear it! You can't live life on the sidelines, and that includes in love."

"Whoa Dad! I didn't say anything about love."

"And I did. On purpose! Check him out. Run a background file. I bet you already have."

She smiled.

"No red flags?"

"Nothing too troubling."

"That's good. I trust your judgment. Have a blast, and see if it lasts!"

 "Okay Dad."

"I'm serious Mira. Don't play cat and mouse games with a man. He will lose interest and move on. If he's worthy of you, and you are genuinely interested, let him get to know you. See where it goes, even if it means falling in love."

"I understand. I'll take your sage advice. Or at least I will consider it. Now can we please change the subject?"

"Of course, Sunshine! Tell me about your next destination!"

Mira was happy to oblige, even as she began to absorb her father's words of advice. Love and matters of the heart were a big deal. She wasn't ready to be that serious, even if Xavier turned out to be the second best man on the planet, after her dad of course.

"Next stop..." Right as she was about to enroll her father into adventures in Costa Rica, Ms. Emma appeared with her breakfast items, and all thoughts of Xavier were displaced by food and travel...

****

Xavier waited for the phone to ring a few more times. He knew his Papa was never near a telephone. Usually it took ten rings as his father didn't believe in voice mail. Xavier knew the assisted living place would call if something was ever wrong, and he often called or stopped by unannounced to see for himself if his father was being treated well.

"Aló."

"Aló Papa!"

"Mi hijo Xavier. How are you? Everything okay?"

197

"Si Papa. I am calling to let you know I am going to Costa Rica for a few days on a nature hike. It will be remote."

"A vacation? You? Why?"

"I met someone, and I'm going on a trip with her."

Xavier knew saying too much to his father would lead to many more questions than he had answers for at this point. And he figured it was time to mention Mira before his brother Matias revealed he met Xavier's woman in Las Vegas. At some point no matter how careful he was, the paparazzi just might notice he was spending time with the same woman. If it got back to Papa he would be upset he was not kept in the loop. That is how he kept being photographed with Dana. Because they had been at the same events, been in the same crowd, the snoops had embellished the story.

"Está bueno!"

"Papa, it's still early yet."

"No, no. If you are mentioning her, and going on a trip together, then there's something special about this one. What's her name and when are you going to bring her to meet your Papa?"

"Really, Papa! It's still early."

"You're stalling. I know she must be stunningly beautiful to get your attention."

"Her name is Mira, and I'm not ready for her to be overwhelmed by our family." Xavier shook his head. His father was the real charmer. At some point he wanted Mira to meet his entire family. As he said, it was still too soon. The only reason Mira had met Matias was because of the *Formula One* race opportunity. He knew his brother would never forgive him if he didn't try to include him since he was such a huge race enthusiast.

"Mira. Sight. I believe would be the English translation of her name. She is very wise to see the goodness in you, my son. It's time for you to trust someone with your heart. You know you're not getting any younger."

Xavier shook his head. "I'd love to carry on with this conversation. And I have to go. I just wanted you to know where I am in case you need anything. "

"I will be fine. Go live your life, and remember what I said. Give yourself a chance to be happy with someone like I was with your Mama. Buenos noches."

"Buenos noches, Papa." Xavier clicked off the phone first because his father would wait until he heard a click before setting the phone down.

Xavier didn't know what tomorrow would hold, and at least he had survived mentioning to his Papa that

Mira was in his life. He hadn't said anything to any of his cousins, Tia Catherine or Tio Antonio. One small step at a time…

Chapter 23

*"Would you tell me, please, which way I ought to go
from here? That depends a good deal on where you
want to get to. I don't much care where.
Then it doesn't matter which way you go."
~ Lewis Carroll, Alice in Wonderland*

Gunacaste, Costa Rica

Looking up from her computer screen, Mira watched
Xavier in the distance kicking a soccer ball around
the beach with some little boys. She heard lots of
giggles as he challenged them to dribble toward the
makeshift goal of two sticks protruding from the
darkened sand. She'd bet he was communicating in
their native tongue. Xavier had asked if he could tag
along on her three-day trip to the North Western
coast of Costa Rica. She said that was fine.
Ironically, he didn't have a place here either. The
resort didn't have two bedroom rooms. Instead, she
was able to get him a king bedroom on the same
hallway, without connected doors. He hadn't put any
pressure on her whatsoever to act on their growing
feelings and she didn't feel compelled to give into her
attraction to him. Mira appreciated that because she
was uncertain about what tomorrow could hold for
them—they were from two totally different worlds.
Plus, being sidetracked on her job was not a welcome
distraction.

As she watched him interact with the youngsters, she
wondered what Xavier's own sons would look like
when he had children. Perhaps curly black hair,

slender like their father, with a mischievous grin that persuaded one to think they too possessed an easy-going demeanor. Xavier was too charming for words and she hoped he didn't pass that onto his future offspring. She exhaled, not wanting to admit she was entranced as well. She turned to stare at nature as she lounged on a beautiful black sand beach at the edge of the *El Mangroove*, a spectacularly maintained boutique resort on the *Gulf of Papagayo*. The water, an emerald-green seemed to shimmer with life. If you walked closer, it looked clear, and then outside this bay, it seemed to be bluer. Mira considered the beach sand to be a brownish hue, versus pure black, and she knew it had more to do with the rich volcanic ash, mountainous rock formations, mangroves and lush scenery at the edge of this rainforest. The active and inactive volcanic activity of this nation was quite spectacular and lent itself to lots of opportunities to explore the natural wonders her clients wanted. The weather was hot and humid even at the water's edge. Once before when she had been here at this same beach, the whole bay was smoky with thick air. She'd learned from asking the locals that it was from burning the sugar cane up in the mountains—an important agricultural crop along with growing and harvesting coffee beans. *Playa Hermosa*, just up the road was the most popular beach, and Mira liked it here more. It was quiet and this hotel had phenomenal staff, restaurants and accommodations.

She adored the heat! Why? Because she was right at the edge of the Pacific Ocean, one had the choice between pool or ocean for a swim. Temperatures back in Florida would not consistently be this warm at this time of year. Later this afternoon, they would escape inside for a traditional Costa Rican coffee grinding and tasting demonstration. And then she hoped for another beautiful sunset—this area of coastline said to be the place to see the best sunsets in the whole of the country. Her phone rang. Looking away from the beach to the phone, she saw the local exchange. Thinking it might be the tour operator, she pressed on switching to Spanish.

"Hola, buenos dias."

It was the tour operator, as expected.   She needed to concentrate. Thus, Mira turned in the chair to put her back to Xavier and the children.

"Si, si." They were confirming the next day's tour up the volcanic mountain in Guanacaste. The man on the other end of the line reiterated the details of the ten-hour tour. The nice thing about this region is it provides for beaches, mountains, and some unique sites. She would see for herself if this hike would deliver for her clients the exotic jungle adventure. If not, she'd choose to go inland to the rainforest to conduct more research.

"Gracias Senor." That was good. Tomorrow, eight in the morning they would leave after breakfast, meeting the guide who would carry them in an open jeep into the brush. She ended the call and she put the phone back on her towel.

"You speak Espanol?"

She nearly jumped out of her seat, not expecting anyone. She'd forgotten all about Xavier playing on the beach.

"Si, mi amigo."

"Why didn't you tell me?" He said stretching his long body onto the beach lounger to her right.

"You didn't ask, and I recognize you hail from Espana," she said trying to stay focused on his question.

"I just assumed you didn't." He smiled, shrugging his shoulders as if being wrong was no big deal.

"An incorrect assumption!" She smiled back appreciating that he was unconcerned about his mistake. "I learned in school. When one is from Florida, Spanish is the water we swim in."

"A very good course correction. Please forgive me."

"There's nothing to forgive. Never assume you know someone is my best advice."

"Speaking from experience?"

"Very much so. People are complex, and complicated. Some can be very misleading."

"Yes, that is true. I would never be that way."

"I'm not suggesting that you would. And you are not

the only person on the planet. I deal with people every day. Not everyone considers others. They think about their interests and damn yours."

"Si, some people are selfish!"

"Well, it's just best to be wary and forewarned."

"That way there's no disappointment?"

"That way you're paying attention and you can adjust in any circumstances."

"I too have learned life rarely goes according to plan."

"Well sometimes it does. I'm a planner. And the conversation you overheard was all about tomorrow's plan coming together."

"What are we doing? Another beach day?"

"Nope, we're going on a mountain adventure!"

"Okay. We're hiking?"

"We're doing it up! We're ziplining, then hiking into the tropical rainforest. There we'll find the natural bridges to cross and waterfalls of *Rincon del la Vieja National Park*. Also, we will go horseback riding, get to experience the natural hot springs and mud baths."

"It sounds amazing. A lot going on in that itinerary."

"Indeed. My clients are nature lovers and want to experience the lush canopy of another rainforest."

"I'm looking forward to it. Do we pack a picnic lunch?"

"Absolutely not. They will provide a traditional Costa Rican lunch."

"Food, water and mud smeared all over us. What's not to love!"

"Yeah , I guess. Mud is a little extra for me. And I'll adjust."

"Chalk it up to just part of the job!"

"Yes. You're here. It will be lots of exercise and fun!"

"That's the spirit. I promise I'll make you laugh all day."

"Deal! Maybe I will schedule a massage for our return."

"Whatever you think is best."

"For today though…more beach relaxation." She sighed laying back on the lounger. Sometimes work required a lot more effort than she wanted. Today was to be relished and tomorrow she'd throw herself into it with gusto when it arrived.

Chapter 24

*"To us, family means putting your arms around each
other and being there."*
~ Barbara Bush

Christmas Day

Jaen, Spain

Christmas gatherings had been going on for days, and
Xavier was antsy. They had finished dinner, and he
was hanging out with his cousins having after dinner
drinks and a smoke. He should have stayed with Papa
in New York, or spent it in Jacksonville to be near
Mira. Even though she was spending time with her
family, perhaps he could have secured a coffee date
or a walk on the beach in the early morning. He'd
enjoyed all his trips watching her work, stealing a
kiss here and there.   One thing for sure, family time
wasn't as exciting without her here.

"Mamma, what are you doing in here?" His cousin,
Juan Carlos, said standing next to the study doors.
"This smoke is not good for you!"

Everyone looked up and stopped their individual
conversations. Tia commanded that kind of respect.
Even though they had gathered for after dinner
brandy and cigars, no one was more important than
the matriarch of their family.

"Just stopping in to say good night. Your Papa has
already retired upstairs."

There was a chorus of: 'Goodnight Mama, and Buenas Noches Tia,' as everyone set aside puffing on their cigars.

"I think you should leave baby Coco here with us, and you and Lacey go off for New Years to have a fabulous second honeymoon. Or go back to Antigua. Perhaps you'll make another baby! Matter of fact, all of you go!" She waved her hand around the room to where her sons and nephews stood. Everyone was very still, suddenly not making eye contact with her. Xavier held his breath.

"It could be a couple's getaway. And all of you could make babies and then they'll be born at the same time. That would be fantastical! We could have group birthdays. I would get Papa to build a new wing on the Palazzo."

"Mama that's ridiculous! We can't just leave Coco and go away." Juan Carlos chimed in.

"Yes you can! The nanny can help me just like she helps you."

"I'll discuss it with Lacey." His cousin seemed resigned to giving his mother her way.

"So what you're saying is, 'Go Away!'"

"Never Mama!"

"Well anyway, every one of you should take seriously my advice. Buenos Noches, my loves."

When the door closed, no one immediately spoke. It was not beneath Tia Catherine to return for the last, last word. When nothing happened, Juan Carlos spoke up.

"I would have thought Lacey and I bought you all some time in having Coco. Clearly that is not the case. Good luck my brothers!" He said laughing and he raised his glass.

Xavier thought that his queue to escape. "I will leave you Gutiérrez men to strategize. I am calling it a night."

"The night is young Xa. Why are you leaving?"

"The night is not young for me. I am flying back to the States in the morning to visit with Papa." He heard grumbles. He hugged all his cousins and escaped out a side door into the cold night.

When he got in his car, he opened his phone and dialed Mira's number. He had memorized it weeks ago. After five rings, her voicemail picked up. When the beep sounded, he said, "Hi Mira, Mira, Merry Christmas! Wish I was there for a walk on the beach with you. Enjoy and call me when you have time." He clicked off, figuring she might be immersed in family traditions as he had been as well. Even though she hadn't answered, he hoped she would know he was thinking about her.

****

Mira pulled into her driveway at about five in the evening on Christmas Day. It had been a full day, and all she wanted was a hot shower and a glass of wine. Church, serving food for the less fortunate at the shelter and then the annual brunch/gift exchange at her parents' house had kept her out since seven this morning. She'd shut her phone off at dawn so she wouldn't be distracted by a myriad of text messages being sent on such a festive holiday. She had friends and associates all over the world and this was one of those pretty universal holidays. Not that she wasn't appreciative of all the well wishes, it could just be overwhelming. Her parents had always stressed to look out for the less fortunate, and that was the center of her day's plan. She especially enjoyed seeing families have a hearty meal and sharing lots of smiles on the holidays.

Dragging her tired body out of the car, she decided to leave her gifts in the trunk for the evening. There was nothing perishable and the neighborhood was ultra-safe so no one would disturb anything. While she had a home security monitoring system, she could keep her alarm disarmed and even leave her doors unlocked in this community. Mira didn't make a habit of testing fate. Once inside the door, she walked to the back on the house where the kitchen opened up to a large set of windows. She turned the phone on and set it on the white countertop. All the buzzing from the messages could be distracting. And priority one, get a glass and take the opened bottle of wine from the refrigerator. As she poured, the buzzing continued. After a couple sips of her favorite white wine, she picked up the phone. She could see she had a voicemail message.

I hope it is not a work call. I am not in the mood, she spoke aloud. She hit the voicemail message and the speakerphone. The voice that came through was the familiar thick accented object of her desire: Xavier.

"Hi Mira, Mira, Merry Christmas! Wish I was there for a walk on the beach with you. Enjoy and call me when you have time."

That was such a sweet gesture from him! She looked over to the microwave clock. It was ten past five in Florida and Spain was six hours ahead. She wasn't sure if he'd still be celebrating with family or sleeping. She shifted from one foot to the other. *Slow down Mira.* She took another sip of wine. Then she had an idea. She picked up the phone and opened her messaging app:

> *"Merry Christmas Xavier and thanks for your message. I too, would have loved to have been walking on the beach with you today. I'm worn out, and it's late. Let's talk tomorrow when you land safely back in New York. Sweetest of dreams and I hope all your Christmas wishes came true!"*

She pressed the send button, and set the phone down. She didn't care about any other messages. She picked up her glass of wine and walked over to the floor to ceiling windows. This was her favorite part of the house. Her simple four bedroom home sat on the fourteenth hole of a golf course, with lush greens and hills outside for her perusal and enjoyment. Many wanted to be on the ocean, or a waterway. Mira didn't. She preferred land over water. She heard the phone buzz. Could it be Xavier? She crossed back around the table to where her phone sat. She picked it up and it awakened.

> *"My dream just came true when you wished me Merry Christmas! Sweetest of dreams Mira, Mira.*
>
> *Goodnight, you charmer!"* She responded.

He send an emoji face with a wink.

She smiled to herself. Today was now complete and perfect.

Chapter 25

*"Trust is the glue of life. It's the most essential
ingredient in effective communication. It's the
foundational principle that holds all relationships."*
~ Steven Covey

Early January

The first two weeks of January went by in a
whirlwind. Business meetings had picked up, and
Mira felt like everyone was a demand for her time,
including Xavier. Just now, he'd brought her a
surprise lunch. Her trusted assistant Miguel and
Xavier had been conspiring again. She wasn't
unhappy about it because she really wanted to spend
more time with Xavier.

"I have a surprise for you!" He said as he sat next to
her in the conference room.

She set the fork down. It had been midway between
her mouth and plate. It held the first bite of her
favorite, *Key Lime Pie*. She tried to keep the next
words she spoke on an even tone.

"I don't like surprises, Xavier."

"You'll like this one! I promise!"

She folded her hands on top of the napkin that sat on
her lap. He continued on as she fascinated herself
with the delicate cream filling that sat atop the
graham cracker crust. She'd eaten *Key Lime Pie*

many times over the years, and her favorite dessert was the *'raisin de etre'…'the reason to be'* as the French say.

"I'm taking you to St. Thomas at week's end for a few days."

"What?" She looked up from the pie, searching his eyes for explanation. "Xavier, I can't just leave!"

"Yes you can!" She saw the determination, the challenge.

"Why do you think I can up and disappear?" All sense of calmness had left her.

"You own the business! You can get away for some real R&R."

"But I have arrangements to make! Now is not the time for rest, and I have no interest in relaxing," which Mira knew wasn't exactly the truth.

"You're stressed out and I'm serious. If there is something urgent that arises, arrangements can be made from there."

"Wow, you are being serious! I appreciate the gesture and politely decline." She returned her stare to the uneaten slice of pie, not wanting him to see how excited she was at just the thought of him considering her well-being and demanding her escape. At first, she'd thought to tune him out and consume her favorite dessert. This one guilty pleasure in her day, and nothing else. She wanted to get away and unwind. Who wouldn't? Business was good right now and as tempting as a weekend getaway with no work sounded, with him anywhere on the planet—she could not afford to ignore her clients.

"Mira? Look at me!" She slowly let her eyes find his once again. She saw the challenge they held for her to balk at him. She waited for him to say whatever had made him ask her emphatically to pay attention.

"A few days is all I'm asking. A secluded resort on the beach. I know just the place."

"Oh you've been there before with other women?"

"Not at all. You will not goad me into changing the subject nor my mind. I was reading a travel blog, and *Frenchman's Reef* just opened up again after a five-year renovation of the property."

"I know the place. I've set up trips there in the past."

"Yes well, the newly launched *Bouy Haus* is waiting for us."

"I wish I could go, and I have too much work to do!"

"A few nights will upset nothing. I can see bridezilla is creating a lot of last minute upsets."

He was talking about Anna Pavlon, a very ritzy socialite that she'd been working with for the last few months. Anna's long-term beau, Michel Richon—a wealthy venture capitalist, proposed to her on the last day of their vacation at a French chateau in the Loire Valley.

"Yes well the couple deserve the best wedding day. Anna means well. And everything is almost rearranged. She only needs to now find a pastry chef who's available to make her dream cake in Barcelona instead of in St. Tropez."

"You're better than me. Six weeks before the destination wedding is too late to change the venue to another country, no less."

She waved nonchalantly. "Twists and turns are the nature of the business and I'm well compensated!"

"That's crap Mira. Peace of mind is everything!"

"Really Xavier? Respect my business! They'll be married before long. I'll get paid, there'll be rave reviews and a long list of future clients from this headache."

"Say you don't need a respite? When was the last time you went anywhere you weren't working?"

She pursed her lips. She had no answer. She felt trapped in a snare.

"Exactly my point! You can't even remember!"

"Let me think for a minute?" She picked up her fork once more, this time pushing the uneaten morsel in her mouth. She could lose herself in this pie, even while she felt his intense stare.

After a couple minutes of awkward silence, she nonchalantly said, "I really can't remember."

"Mira, I'm putting my foot down. Thursday morning, the charter jet will whisk us off to St. Thomas for three nights. Either you'll pack clothes or you can spend the weekend in nothing but a robe. That is your choice."

She mulled over their conversation. Was it worth the argument? She really did need a few days of pampering and rest. She was grateful to Xavier for noticing and demanding she pay attention.

"Fine! You win, I'll go!"

****

Thursday…

He stepped off the chartered plane first. And then he held out his hand for her. She took it and walked down the five steps onto the tarmac in St. Thomas, United States Virgin Islands at half past ten in the morning. They'd had a relatively quick three-and-half hour flight coming from Jacksonville. Mira didn't care. She was excited to have a few days to unwind. Miguel had rearranged her schedule and she had no calls or meetings for the rest of the week. Of course Mira expected if there was an emergency,

Miguel would reach out. He'd promised he would and nothing would happen.

"The car is over there," Mira watched Xavier point his finger to the edge of the row of private jets. She saw a black sedan with tinted windows, and a friendly looking driver who seemed to know he was picking them up.

"Couldn't we have just rented a vehicle?"

"No querida. That would stir a natural curiousness for you to explore. This is not a research trip. You are relaxing and I get to be the observer to make sure it happens."

"Fine! I already promised no work!"

"Si, you did. The driver will deposit us at the resort, and if you need something, I will get it for you."

"Now being catered to by you, I could get used to."

"We'll see if you really mean that!" He said pausing to look at her as they walked towards the sedan.

She decided not to respond further. As they resumed walking, she felt the heat of his hand on her back gently guiding her forward to the waiting car.

"Mr. Gutiérrez and Ms. Morales, welcome to paradise! My name is Peter, and I am at your service. I've provided cold drinks in the vehicle. Our ride will be approximately twenty-five minutes around through town and over onto the hill at Frenchman's

Reef. There might be a little traffic as we go through town. This is our rush hour on a working day."

Xavier extended his hand to the driver. "Very nice to meet you, Peter. We're glad to be here!" Mira just smiled. She didn't like being catered to, preferring to control her comings and goings on her own time. And she wouldn't complain. It was one less detail she didn't need to work out.

Peter opened the door, and she climbed in first. Then Xavier slid into the seat next to her. She could feel the heat emanating off his body even in the cool interior. His leg rubbed against hers and all she could think about was putting her hand out to touch him. She thought it best not to create an incident, so she kept her hands in her lap.

"Thank you for taking care of all the little details." She could appreciate him.

"My pleasure, querida."

They rode in silence looking out the window at all the scenes of this mountainous paradise. The water spanned from deep blue, to turquoise, as it shimmered with the sun. As promised, exactly twenty-five minutes later they pulled up in front of an open air building that said, *Morningstar Buoy Haus* in the luxury brand for a popular hotel chain. Mira knew the place from brochures. It had just been renovated after the hurricane a few years back that had destroyed it. Along with the sister hotel, *Westin*, up the hill.

Before Peter could come around and open the door, Xavier had opened it and escaped the vehicle. He was a control freak too! He held a hand out for her, and she took it as she placed her sandaled feet on the cement at the edge of the beautiful landscape. Everywhere she looked there were flowers, palm trees and inviting seas.

"It looks so beautiful here!"

"They say it is one of the prettiest areas of the island." As she turned and looked at all the different angles, Xavier and Peter sorted their luggage. In the distance, she could see the beach on the other side of what looked to be a restaurant. To the right side of this building there was a row of low-level white washed buildings, two stories in height. Mira assumed those were the villas. Again, she and Xavier hadn't talked about sleeping accommodations, and she wasn't concerned at all.

"Do you want to come into reception, or stay out here?"

"Would it be okay if I walked over there?" Mira pointed to an open courtyard that was lined with low-level bushes.

"You can do whatever you desire. I will check us in and meet you there."

"Thank you."

"Mira, you don't have to keep saying thank you to me for doing something nice."

"I want to! I'm grateful!"

He simply nodded, and then turned and walked into the building. On the left, as she watched him, she could see some desks positioned in an alcove—very unassuming reception area. She walked in the opposite direction, up the two steps, and then another five steps into and out of the building, which landed her into an open air courtyard. Low bushes enclosed a human-sized chessboard, with pieces that were as large as her legs. Just beyond, the space gave way to an amazing unobstructed view of the beach and Caribbean Sea. Mira briefly closed her eyes, and exhaled. *Relax yourself,* she chanted silently.

"We're all set." Mira heard from just behind her.

"That was fast!" She said opening her eyes and turning towards him in the same moment.

"Si, they just wanted my identification. This is our oasis for the next three days. Our villa is further down the walkway. We can walk there or get a golf cart ride. You choose?"

"I would prefer to walk. It will help me acclimate to being here. Do they bring our luggage?"

"Si. Let's walk." He held out his hand and she placed hers into his.

"It seems so quiet here. I like it."

"I picked it because this is the least crowed resort and it has a beach. The hotel up the hill is very busy. I made you a spa appointment there though for later this afternoon."

"What?"

"Yes, spa. All arranged and paid for!"

"I don't need to go to the spa. The beach is relaxing enough! Plus, how do you know I would like the spa?"

He stopped walking and turned to her. "Mira, I was serious...we are here so you focus on wellness, restoration, relaxation. Just as you listen to me, I listen to you. I know you like the spa. I remember that conversation we had."

"But…"

He placed his finger over her lips. "Just listen," he requested and waited.

She shook her head up and down, and let out another relaxing breath. He spoke again.

"The description said it is a '*Heavenly Spa*,' with relaxation lounge. They even serve cups of herbal tea and homemade lavender chamomile cookies. The photos are quite impressive. The relaxation room has plush chaise lounges with a view of the Charlotte Amalie town harbor."

"Sounds like you really did some research. How can I argue."

"I know a massage will force you to relax. I signed you up for something called the *"Heavenly Spa Ritual."*

She giggled. "I'm not sure I have ever heard a man know the details of a spa treatment."

"There's more… The goal is to reach a state of bliss...as part of the three stone ritual, you will be asked to set your intention and choose a stone based on what you would like to think about during the treatment. The stones are inspired by "something you are hoping for, something you are grateful for, and someone you love."

"Wow, they really swayed you!"

"Mira, Mira, I expect you to walk out of there fully relaxed. That is my only request. And I will ask you when you return if you accomplished that goal."

"You're not coming to get a little 'slice of heaven' too?" She said using air quotes.

"Heavens no! If I were that close to you, I would not be interested in spa or relaxing. I would be ready to devour you."

"But…"

"No buts, Mira," he said putting his finger to her lips once more. "It's all been arranged. Now let's find our villa, number eight."

He continued to walk them the rest of the way down the path to where he must have been told to find Villa Eight. She tottered along a step behind him as he turned the corner into the foliage, where the concrete path split. The trail continued as if they were about to walk onto the sand and then the sea. Bushes full of lush green and fuchsia-colored bougainvillea flowers were in full bloom, brown colored crab grass and some splattered palm trees—all of it giving a glimpses of the sea a mere sixty feet down a slight decline to the water's edge. They were separated by a concrete path and white metal decorative fence curving around the corner.

"Wow, the water has to be at least four shades of blue, from deep navy to aquamarine, and then to the height of a turquoise blue mixed in the middle." Mira wasn't sure if Xavier had even stopped to listen to her or if he'd gone ahead. Looking down near the shore she could see the water presented as a blue-green, almost clear, iridescence that reminded her of the Maldives. She wanted to go jump in, fully clothed. Slowly she tore her eyes away, to pick up her pace again to see where Xavier had ended up. She found him on the backside of the path that ended at a white building, with a matching white door, and silver door handle. On the right side, just above the doorway, there was a lamp light, and sign that read #8. She pushed the partially open door walking in.

"There you are. I was wondering where you had stopped." He said across the room.

"I was just admiring the view."

"This view is ours," he turned to move out of the way of the shuttered patio doors in their living room. She could see a balcony with a table, two chairs, and a swing, enclosed by a more white metal fencing that was only waist-high. She walked closer and there she could see the open beach, with millions of grains of white sand, a few trees peppering the distance, and water that shimmered with calm laps and gentle waves.

"This is spectacular! It also looks secluded."

"Glad you can appreciate both together. Even though we know this is not as secluded as the Maldives, it will not be overrun with beachgoers. I am convinced you will have no issue relaxing here!"

"I'll be more than fine." She looked around the room in shades of white and tan—a couch, two oversized chairs, a wide screen television mounted on the wall, a low coffee table and space carpet covering the tiled floors. There was also a mini refrigerator, glassware, and coffee maker. The standard room amenities and very well maintained.

"Your bedroom is over there, and mine is next to it," he said as he pointed to the other side of where they stood.

"Outdoor bathroom here?"

"No, we each have our own, both indoor and air conditioned facilities."

"Bummer! No garden in the humid midst!"

"Less lizards to watch!"

"That's a very convincing argument which means I will like it better here! Thanks for thinking of everything!"

"My pleasure. Let's go check out the rest of the resort, so you are all settled in for your treatment later."

"Can we eat first?"

"Of course. I forgot that we haven't eaten. Reception said there's an open-air restaurant next to the pool and ocean on this end of the resort. Let's go see if they have space for us."

"Now that sounds heavenly!"

"Agreed." He went to the door and opened it for you. "After you, Senorita."

Mira glided through the door, almost floating on the idea of doing little or nothing with Xavier making all the arrangements. A new experience for her, one she could get used to enjoying.

****

Xavier had been correct. The spa, with its subtle sand and stone colored tones was the epitome of serenity. She'd chosen to walk up the stairs from their resort on the lower end of the hill to get in some exercise. She could have caught the shuttle bus up the hill, and the view wasn't as pretty from the road as it was from the beach. Mira would have considered what they called hills, to instead be steep mountains. Because she hailed from Florida she had a different interpretation of nature. While she supposed that the locals were very used to their climate, she could feel the burn in her calves and thighs—evidence she had indeed gotten a workout.

When Mira arrived to the *Westin Resort* a few hours prior, she walked into the spacious lobby that was full of neutral tones, accentuated by darker wood accepts. High above the sea and town below, the backside provided spectacular views. The front desk noted that the spa was on pool level below, and she could either walk down the massive staircase or take the elevator. She opted for the elevator, ready to get off her spaghetti legs. Walking through the double doors into the spa, she was welcomed with open arms and lots of pleasant smiles. She had been ushered into the ladies' lounge area to undress, put on a plush robe and rubber slippers. Then she was escorted to

the serenity room, where she was offered to partake
in herbal tea and cookies. It was just as Xavier had
described. There were lots of other choices too, and
she was happy to keep it simple. The view of the
pool, and the town of Charlotte Amalie sitting in the
midst of the hills, booming with life—both by sea
and land, was gorgeous. In the distance, she could
see homes built on cliffs overlooking the sea. It all
seemed pretty calm and sunny today. She tempered
her breathing, and closed her eyes, basking in this
moment. *Mira, you have the best life.* Just as Mira
felt herself drifting off to sleep, she heard a voice
calling her name. Snapping to attention, Mira
realized it was time for her treatment.

****

After an amazing massage, Mira was again returned
back to the relaxation room, where she sipped on
more tea, and took a short nap. When she awoke—
buffed, restored and polished, she felt like she didn't
have a care in the world. She got dressed, and took
the leisurely walk downhill on the road, still feeling
this paradise was bliss! As she walked, she reflected
on what the therapist had asked before her treatment:
what did she want to focus on? She taken the safe
route—to meditate on something she was grateful
for. She was grateful for her life, and most especially
for Xavier's awareness that she was at a high level of
stress. She was also grateful for the time they were
taking to share priceless moments together. Mira
wasn't a fan of hoping; she was more of a doer. And
she was almost afraid to think about Xavier and the
"L" word. She suspected she was falling or had

fallen in love with him. That was somewhat scary though. He seemed like a really great guy. Could she trust herself? She did believe what he told her, even about his infamous past, present scrutiny and popularity. Hadn't she already let him in? She'd never let someone tag along while she worked, let alone allow them to take care of her mental and emotional needs. Maybe she would take some time over these next few days to figure out what she really wanted. Did she see a higher level of commitment with him? Perhaps her parents had been right. It was time to decide. Mira could feel the tension start to invade her neck and shoulders. *No, no, no, we are not going to undo the work of that blissful massage. Enjoy the moment Mira*, she whispered to herself as she re-entered the *Buoy Haus* property. Mira couldn't wait to tell Xavier about her exquisite spa experience.

She walked along the path pausing to touch or sniff a flower, here or there. What was that saying? '*Stop and smell the roses*.' Wouldn't be long before sunset. Mira wasn't sure what their dinner plans would be, and she was starving.

Mira walked into their villa and Xavier was sitting on the couch with remote in hand. On the television was a soccer game. She had come to realize he was a big fan of the sport. He turned the volume to mute, as she closed the door.

"Hello Gorgeous! How was it?" She noticed he was sitting there in casual linen slacks, and a white button up shirt. He had a perpetual tan with olive hues because of his Spanish heritage. No additional sunbathing required.

"Divine and delicious! That was the best few hours ever, ever! My body feels like marshmallows."

"Marshmallows? I do not know this term."

"Like soft, but solid. Really, I'm relaxed."

"Si. Good. That was the goal!"

"Absolutely! Mission accomplished. Thank you for the treat!"

"My pleasure, querida."

"What have you been up to?"

"Not much. I had a few business calls. I've watched a couple futbol games. And I checked on Papa who says he wants to meet the woman who keeps me in paradise." He laughed.

"I'm sure. I would like to meet him as well. I probably do not want to go to New York this time of year."

"I understand, sunshine seekers find little joy in New York in January. Many spend the winters in the South I am told."

"Oh yes, the snow birds who come for the winter.
We see that with all the license plates from the
Northern States."

"I do not know that I have ever noticed."

"When I was a child my parents and I would play
games of guessing the next state license plate we
would see on the highways. It passed the time."

"I will pay closer attention when we are back on the
mainland."

"Who's winning your game?" Mira pointed to the
television.

"No one. It is still tied zero-zero."

"And that is fun to watch?"

"Si, very much so. There are strategies upon
strategies to get eleven people to work together and
outguess the goalie of the other team. Anyway, that is
not what I want to talk about."

"Oh?"

"Do you want to have dinner at *Isla Blue*, the
restaurant on the second floor above reception, or
would you like room service? I made a reservation
for seven just in case. They said the restaurant has a
great menu."

"Let's go to the restaurant. I saw photos of it with its white décor, curtains, glass chandeliers, and circle lantern lights. It looks very quaint. Plus, it seems like it is going to be a lovely evening outside."

"Your wish is my command!"

"We are in paradise so we might as well soak it up, right?"

"Indeed!"

"Go back to watching your game. I am going to go take a shower and get ready."

"Need any help scrubbing your back? I would be happy to oblige so you do not lose your mush feeling."

"Very good use of that term. And no, I'm good!" She said laughing. She knew if they ended up in the shower together there would be no leaving the room.

"Let me know if you change your mind."

"I definitely will not be changing my mind." Mira turned and went in the opposite direction, excited that he'd thought of dinner plans. She had the perfect dress for tonight—a shimmering blue maxi dress, with spaghetti straps, a scoop neck and side split. She'd brought some iridescent white, low-heeled wedge sandals that were very comfortable, and an opaque sheer wrap with sequins to match. None of it too fancy, and yet a little extra for a night out in paradise. She had thought being with an international

companion might require her to pay closer attention
to how she looked on his arm.

****

Mira emerged from her room wearing what looked to
be a second skin in blue. She was breathtakingly
beautiful and that dress was elegant and provocative.
Xavier's mouth dropped open, and he cleared his
throat.

"You look stunning, Mira." He said as he got up from
the couch, pressed the off button on the game, and set
the remote on the table.

"It must be the amazing massage I had earlier. If you
feel good, you look good!"

"No, it's you. You are beautiful, always. And that
dress, compliments your figure, your hair and your
eyes. It reminds me of the water outside."

She giggled. "Have I mentioned how charming you
are, Mr. Gutiérrez?"

"You might have, and I'm serious!" He crossed the
small space to stand before her. He put his finger
under her chin to tilt her head up so she could see that
he was being truthful. She blinked at him unwilling
to break the silence. He'd noticed that about her. She
had a measured patience that would test the best of
minds.

"You are the most beautiful woman I have ever seen!
Ever wanted. You are a complete package of mind,

233

body and goodness. Very alluring and unassuming is a devastating combination. I could stare at you all night in this dress. May I touch you?"

She shook her head.

He had to be sure. "Say it?"

"Yes, please touch me Xavier."

He pulled her into his arms, committed to touch the fabric that held her so skillfully in place, with enough exposed skin to entice him to feel where there was no fabric. She smelled of lavender and vanilla. He leaned his lips down to hers so he could taste her too. Just one small kiss, and then they would go to dinner. She put her hands his chest, and he felt every inch of her as she wove her hands up to touch his neck, his hair. Xavier lost focus on reality and he felt the soft glide of her smooth skin at the same time their mouths dueled for more, more, more. One rational thought crossed his mind to bring back an ounce of control to his unbridled passion for her.

"Mira, we need to stop!" He said on an exasperated whisper.

She blinked back at him, as she looked momentarily confused.

"I've reached the point where if I go any further, I will be taking you to bed, not dinner."

He sensed she was debating with herself. "You're right. We got carried away. It was nice though."

He decided not to inquire into her nice comment. They both had been caught up in the moment. And he needed her to be sure about bed or dinner.

"Dinner," he heard her exhale, resigning himself to a frustrated night that he would mentally enjoy regardless if they didn't have sex.

"Si. Let's go to dinner. Our reservation awaits." He stepped away from her and headed to the door to open it for her. He watched as she picked up her small purse and wrap and swept by him out the opened doorway. He got a whiff of her subtle scent again. *Dios mio, she was going to be the death of him.*

Chapter 26

"Desire is the starting point of all achievement, not a hope, not a wish, but a keen pulsating desire which transcends everything." ~ Napoleon Hill

The next day…

They had just made it inside from the beach before the downpour. In quick time the sunny skies turned into dark clouds, and their time by the water was shortened by an impending storm, at least for now.

"That was close!" Mira said as they closed the door on buckets of rain starting to drench everything that was not covered.

"We were wet enough from the water." Xavier said as if it was no big deal.

"Ha, you think so? I'm not so sure." Mira laughed.

"Let's go out to the patio to watch the rain. It's covered, so we should be okay. I love the rain!"

"Me too! Especially, if I'm not soaked and cold."

"You want another towel to take with us?" He asked.

"No, I'm going to put on a sun dress and get a blanket."

"Okay," he said picking up a dry beach towel and heading outside.

When Mira emerged out onto the patio, she noticed
he was sitting on the swing that was suspended from
the ceiling. It looked like a bee hive made of wicker
woven wood, with a cutout for comfort. On the seat
was a soft, thick cushion. The patio was simple in
décor, other than the swing. It had two brown
matching wicker chairs, and a small table between
them. Some balconies at the resort had couches.
Even though they had greenery all around to give a
sense of privacy, the centerpiece of everything was
the sea that spread out less than one hundred feet in
front of them just beyond the sandy beach. The
downpour made visibility into the distance almost
impossible, even as the still darkening skies
threatened to bring even more intense rain.

"Come over here with me where it's dry? I'll keep
you warm," he said gently swinging.

Mira thought that was a great idea as she closed the
sliding door behind her so the air conditioning would
not cut off. She walked the three steps to stand
before him. He lifted her and placed her across his
lap as if she weighed nothing. Then he wrapped them
both in the soft blanket she held. It would shelter
them from any residual sprays of the driving,
sideways rain.

"We can snuggle and watch the downpours."

"Si. Over there the storm is moving." She looked
over to where he pointed.

“I know that the rains come and go. And even though I love the rain, I don’t really like storms.”

“Mira, Mira, the storms of life will always come. If you prepare for them, there is nothing to fear.”

“Why do I get the impression you are talking about more than just the rain?”

“It is the way of nature with all things. Life ebbs and flows. We must always continue to learn to go beyond just surviving to thrive. Sometimes we are outscored in this moment. Then when the next moment comes, we could be better prepared to play to win.”

“I get it. I do that a lot in business.”

“What about in life other than business? What about us, Mira?”

“What do you mean?”

“Are you going to give us a chance to thrive?”

“I’m ready to give us a chance, Xavier.”

She leaned in and gave him a quick kiss on the lips. Then she leaned in and touched her tongue to his lips.

“Mira, you are playing with fire! You already know what you do to me. We’re here snuggling, and I have a tight control in place. You can’t tease me!”

"I want you! I want us! I want this!" She gave him another kiss on the lips.

"You want to make love?"

"Yes!"

"Let's go inside."

"No! Here, now!" What she finally admitted to herself she was now determined to have.

"Now? Here?" She heard him repeat her words.

She kissed him outright making no mistake about what she wanted in answer to his question. She touched his chest and her hand started to move downward.

"Mira…"

"Hmmm," she said kissing his neck.

"You gotta keep still if I'm going do this properly."

"Do I?" she said. She moved her hand down further still to reach the drawstring of his swim trunks.

"Oh damn! Woman, stop!"

"No!"

She pulled him free, and rubbed her hands over the hard smooth skin of his manhood. She heard him groan, which emboldened her more so. Lifting her head from his neck, she whispered in his ear. "You want me to stop?"

"Hell no, you minx!"

She kissed him again, tongues dueling and the heat rising between them. She began stroking him faster. She moved her legs to straddle him. Feeling the swing rocking was a pure turn on. No one knew that they were outside in the rain about to have sex. She pulled up the blanket and her dress.

"Mira, what are you doing?"

"Put your hands here." She guided him to place a hand on each side of hips. Then as she found her way back to his slick manhood, she guided him to slide inside her aching vagina.

"Let me protect us. I wasn't planning…" He mumbled against her lips.

"Shhhhh! Trust me. I'm a step ahead. On birth control." She rose up and came down again so he would get the picture. She put her arms around his neck and kissed him again. She was going to ride him until they both reached orgasm.

He gave a low growl. "You are pure temptation!"

"I think the word for today is bliss."

"You're going too fast. Our first time…Mira, please." She kept up her assault. "I'm going to come if you don't slow down."

"That's exactly what I want." She felt the immediacy of his fighting to hold onto control as their bodies meshed together. This was the best, watching him about to let go for her!

"But, I can't…"

"Stop talking Xavier, and enjoy! I promise this will not be the last time…" And Mira put her lips over his once more as she focused on bringing him immense pleasure without being so noisy. She knew this was the first of many times they would make love. Seconds later and he went over the edge, as she felt him release himself inside her. It was so sexy that it made her orgasm and cling to him.

They were both wet. Not from the rain as one might have thought. Instead from the sweat that had their bodies slick. As the sensations slowed, Mira lifted her head from his chest.

"Was that okay?" She said searching his eyes. Rarely did she feel less than confident about the moves she made. She didn't want him to think she was trying to trick him into sex.

"Okay? Dios mio, that was amazing!" He leaned in and kissed her. After a few more kisses, she pulled back.

"Really? You sure? I swear I wasn't thinking this would happen out here. And it was what I wanted."

"I swear back, Mira. I just wanted to hold you. And I wanted you as much as you wanted me. I am the one who should ask if that was okay. It was not my idea of a first time for us."

"It was awesome! You ready for a second time? And maybe a third?"

"Hell yeah! And not out here. I'm going to take you to my bed, strip you of all your clothes and make love to you properly!"

"I thought you'd never ask!"

He righted her clothes and his own. Then lifted her as if she weighed nothing, and carried her back into their villa. He was determined to make sure no one was watching as he devoured her and gave her numerous mind-blowing orgasms. Just maybe the rest of this trip would be spent in bed, which was just fine with him!

Chapter 27

The man who goes alone can start today, but he who travels with another must wait till that other is ready.
~ Henry David Thoreau

St. Augustine, FL

Walking hand in hand on the St. Augustine beach, he looked above Mira's head out at the endless ocean's deep blue waves. The salt water floating on the wind, the sand ever sinking between his barefoot toes, and his hair gently blowing as the sun began to impose it rays in an ascent into the high sky. It was a new day—Saturday in fact, and their leisurely breakfast in bed had stretched into this idea of taking a walk. Enjoying their slow morning of togetherness time—this was living! Or so it seemed. He had adjusted to being in his new home, that opened up to the ocean every morning, regardless of the weather. It was sometimes calm, and sometimes a tempest was raging.   He felt the same way, recognizing he still wasn't settled. It had been three weeks since they returned from St. Thomas. Now that he had claimed her, he wanted more.

He thought this moment to be as good of a time as any to take their relationship to the next level. He had expressed his love for her in his actions, even though he hadn't said it. This was so new to him. By no means was it a controlled passion that he had. He was on fire— consumed by being in Mira's presence. He definitely enjoyed being in her company, their travels had added spice to the mundane existence he had felt while living in New York, and he always looked forward to what she would do next. A spontaneous free spirit is how he would describe her—nothing was impracticable with her. From cycling in the Pyrenees to sunbathing on Costa del Sol, he had never questioned his adventurous spirit, until he met Mira who considered the world as her oyster. Even his family had noticed he had found himself being somewhat blue in mood when he was not around her. *El efecto Mira*, translated in English as '*the Mira effect*,' they now called it! Papa had mentioned that he was dating a woman named Mira. His cousins even joking so much that Tia Catherine had questioned him—who is she, this woman who has taken all your attention? All he could answer was, a woman like no other, and I can't wait for you to meet her!

"Hey, you okay?" She had stopped to ask.

"Si, of course." He continued to walk, and she followed along in step with him.

"You seem deep in thought?"

"Lo siento. I do not mean to be distant. I am thinking."

"Do I want to ask?"

"I don't know. And I have to be honest with you, querida," he said stopping mid-stride.

She said nothing, not letting go of his hand. She was patiently waiting for him to say more.

"What are we? I mean are we boyfriend and girlfriend?"

"Why do we have to put a label on this? On us?" She said wiggling the index finger of her free hand to annotate it was the two of them.

"Because I want you exclusively to myself!"

"You have me already. Do I have to say it to you?"

"Si, and more importantly you have to say it out loud so you hear it yourself! Claim me, claim us?"

"You are an impossible man!"

"No, I am simply a man in love. Someone who is demanding you to say this is important to you."

"Yes, it is important. You are important to me, Xavier. There is no one else, and I do not plan to have anyone else. My business demands my attention too much. You and I are on solid ground."

"I am not questioning that. I see how you look at me, and how you come to pieces in my arms."

"What then is your concern?"

"I want the whole world to know I love you, and that you love me. I want my family to see you fight for an us to be in existence."

"Yes, well it is only important to me that you know. My actions should speak volumes to you. You are welcome to tell anyone."

"Oh, I tell everyone. And I want to know how you feel about it?"

"I am fine with it. I am just not very gooey in emotions."

"Gooey? I do not know this term. It sounds like something of a candy?"

"Sort of. It means soft and sticky, like maybe fruit."

He tilted his head, trying to wrap his head around this term. "I do not think you are gooey at all. You are firm, and strong. Perhaps curvy."

She laughed. "Are you trying to seduce me?"

"Perhaps…is it working?"

"Only if the touchy feely, gooey relationship-labeling talk is over."

"Si. I just want to ensure I express my feelings with you. I have fallen in love with you. I love you Mira, Mira. It is hard for me too; and with you I am trying to do things different than in my past. To do them the right way, and not be closed off. I trust you. Including with my feelings."

"I understand. Really, I do. Let's just enjoy this moment. No labels, no pressure, no upsets. Okay?"

"Si, let's go get ice cream so I can lick gooey off of you…"

"In public?" She giggled.

He liked hearing her giggle. "Perhaps only from your lips outside the house."

"And inside the house?"

"From everywhere off your naked body."

"Oh my…that's steamy!"

"No, the ice cream will be cold!"

"Trust me, I'm already heating up very fast."

"It is my desire to please you," Xavier said so seductively Mira felt like she could faint.

"Let's get back to the subject at hand. Ice cream! What's your favorite flavor?"

"Chocolate, of course."

"What if I don't like chocolate?" She mused.

"Si, this is good! The more for me. I do not have to share mine. Plus, I do not want you to lick it off yourself…it is my desire to lick it off you."

"You are incorrigible! I thought we were going to keep this conversation respectable."

"Si, okay. What is your favorite flavor…of ice cream?"

"Pistachio almond."

"Then we will find both yours and mine and go back to bed! This is turning into the best day ever!"

"Indeed!"

This conversation hadn't exactly gone the way he'd wanted. And he'd leave it for now. At least Mira knew how he felt. And he really did want to take ice cream to bed with his beloved.

****

The following day…

Mira rang the doorbell to her parents' house purposely refraining from using the key code. In her hand she held a large mixed bouquet of flowers in all different shades of white. It was her mother's birthday and she wanted to surprise her. Yesterday she'd had the best day with Xavier, even though he was anxious to label their relationship. She was happy to have something else to focus on, at least for a few hours celebrating her mom.

Mira didn't care for flowers. Especially not cut ones. It was like killing off life for a momentary joy that was fleeting at best. Her mother had been trying to cultivate a love of cut flowers in her since she ceased being a toddler. Mira had seen videos of herself crying when her mother cut them. She could hear the repetitious line:

'Flowers live on in us as we bask in the joy of admiring them in their vase; and then there are always new ones—a purity or renewal if you like.'

Mira thought her mother's rationale was ridiculous. Cut them and they start their death march, not able to get on with thriving. However, today wasn't about her. This bouquet was a way to say thank you to her mom for all the effort to get her to being a stable, productive adult.

Mira had reached out to an associate at the wholesale flower market to make this special request. Two dozen mixed stems in her mom's living room colors, with fern greenery that looked full and alive. The smell had overwhelmed her so much she had to pull over and put them in her trunk. She knew her mom would appreciate it considering Mira's disdain for the practice.

"My word child, you forgot the key code again?" Her mom said opening the door.

"Happy Birthday Mom!" Mira pulled the bouquet from behind her back and presented it forward to her mother. She watched her mother's eyes widen in surprise as she put her hand up to her lips.

"Oh Mira, they're so lovely!"

"For you mom. Happy, Happy Birthday!"

"Thank you," she said tentatively, accepting the bouquet. "But why such an extravagant gift?"

"To say thank you for all you've done for me. I love you!"

"I love you too, and these," she said as she tilted the bouquet to sniff their scent. "These are delicious! Come in for tea. I need to find a vase big enough to hold them all."

Mira watched her mother turn away from the wide open door, not the least bit interested in anything other than those flowers. Mira had accomplished her goal. Her mother was so taken with flower arranging and spent hours perfecting her skills. Stepping in and closing the door behind her, she heard her mother call to her dad.

"Papa, come see what Mirasol has brought me!" It was an order, not a request.

Mira hated when her mother used her full first name. And it was her mother's day after all, so she would allow the indulgence and afford a little more latitude. She slowly walked to the back of the house where she knew her mother would be rummaging through the cabinets.

The tea kettle was always plugged in and she could hear the water starting to reach its boiling point. She plopped down at the kitchen table that overlooked the solarium. The day was full of sunshine and lots of light—the benefit of being in Florida for most of the year. Just off the solarium, was an enclosed lanai and a backyard full of green grass and professionally landscaped flowerbeds. Before Mira was born her parents had moved south from New York proclaiming no more harsh winters. They had forged a unique compromise afforded by her dad's law practice. Her mom loved the warmth of the sun, and her dad appreciated central air conditioning. When the house became too chilly, they could leave her dad inside and the two of them could lounge outside.

Mira often wished they had a pool in the backyard when she was growing up. But her parents belonged to the country club less than two miles from their house. It held a world renowned golf course, indoor and outdoor Olympic-sized swimming pools, tennis courts, multiple restaurants, a bar, a hotel with spa and every other amenity one could think should be included. Nothing was missing except solitude. Her mother was a socialite who made sure Mira was involved in all the 'appropriate' groups and social activities. Mira didn't miss that. Now grown and able to exert her own authority over her life, she often declined the charity events and engagements her mother patronized, content to hear the details after the fact or not at all.

"Hello Scoot," her dad said coming into the kitchen. She jumped up to hug him, her favorite person on the planet.

"Hi Dad!"

"Honey, our daughter brought me the most beautiful bouquet ever. I have to get a large vase down to have them all fit."

"It's quite impressive. Good job!" Her dad winked at her.

"Let me help you? I will get the vase. I think I hear the kettle. Why don't you make the tea?" Her dad said.

"If you insist."

Mira knew her mother was pleased her dad came in at the right time. Mira plopped back into her chair.

"What flavor for our steeped tea, Mira? You choose!"

"No mom. It's your day. So you select and I'll love it." That was another item her mom relished and Mira could have cared less about.

"It is a special occasion, so we'll have some of the Oolong Orchid tea your father brought back from China."

"Mom, you don't have to waste the good stuff on my undistinguished palette!"

"Nonsense, you are my precious daughter, my only child. So we will all share together."

"Okay!" Mira knew better than to resist too much.

"Ladies, I am going to take my tea in the study. I have a business call."

"You work too much, Dad!"

"I have to make money to keep your mother in the lifestyle she's accustomed." He said trying to keep a straight face.

"Nonsense, Marc!" Her mother laughed. "I know you want to watch your Sunday morning political shows."

"You know me oh so well!" Mira watched as her mom handed her dad his mug of tea.

"Love you both!" And just like that, he was gone,

leaving her to chat and sip with her mother.

"Here you go my daughter." She watched her mother put the dainty tea cup and saucer in front of her, with a demitasse spoon and matching sugar dish.

"Thanks Mom."

Mira put two spoons of sugar in her cup and stirred slowly. Melting sugar was all in the technique. Her phone buzzed. She pulled it out of her jacket pocket. It was the message she was waiting for, confirming her appointment with a new client the next morning. She responded to the message: "Confirmed and looking forward to it!"

"You're working today?"

"Yes, for a few hours later. I have a new client meeting tomorrow."

"Do you ever slow down?"

"Not really. It's nice to do what I love. Work ebbs and flows." She said remembering Xavier's words of wisdom in St. Thomas.

"Like the tide?"

"I guess," she shrugged in a non-committal affirmative.

"You know Mira, the greatest joy of my life was marrying your father, having you and being settled down."

Mira was holding her breath, waiting for the other shoe to fall. Her mother continued.

"I want that for you too. You're smart, beautiful, loving and resourceful! You will make a great partner!"

"Thanks mom for your confidence in me. Most especially, thanks for loving me."

"How will you ever settle down?"

Determined not to be abrupt and dismissive today, she again shrugged her shoulders as she stared at the patterned wood flooring.

"I'll figure it out. I'm still young. What are you up to with the rest of today?" No way was she going to mention her blossoming relationship with Xavier. At some point she knew she would. She wanted her parents to meet him.

"If you wait too long, it will limit your options. You don't want to be an old maid with no prospects."

Mira was growing frustrated fast. She'd tried to divert her mother from going down this tunnel.

"Okay mom. I understand your concerns. I love you. Now really, what are you up to with the rest of your day?"

"Your dad is taking me to have French food at a bistro we like. They have lavender Crème Brûlée."

Mira exhaled. Her mom had shifted attention away from her thankfully! Food was her mother's forte! Not long after telling Mira what else she planned to order at the restaurant, her mom suggested they go out to the lanai and watch the home and garden channel on cable. Mira jumped at the chance to be distracted and wholeheartedly agreed!

Chapter 28

"Develop an attitude of gratitude, and give thanks for everything that happens to you, knowing that every step forward is a step toward achieving something bigger and better than your current situation."
~ Brian Tracy

The following week

Mira was sitting in her office, talking to Xavier as she made notes for a new client. He was sitting across the conference table looking as relaxed as ever.

"I get so stressed making sure all the details are covered. My neck and shoulders are sore."

"You think you might have anxiety issues? This is not the first time you've let yourself get stressed."

"I don't know. What's your point?" Mira said chewing on the end of a pencil.

"How about you relax?"

"I can't!"

"When's your next meeting?"

"Tomorrow afternoon in Texas when I have to plan a corporate retreat with a client. Hence, why I am only available to go out tonight."

"Okay well we're going to have an early night and I'm going to give you a massage before bed."

"You mean before we make love?"

"No, I mean before you get a good night's sleep!"

"You will beg me!"

"While I am a weak man around you, that is only when I allow myself to give in."

"Fine!" She wasn't upset with him. "Don't you have work to do? Are you sure that you should have cut your day short to come here?"

"Always there is work. My job is to continue to expand our footprint in North America. I'm mobile too for the most part. That's how I could move my dad to Florida for winters. I will go to New York to check on Papa while you're in Texas."

"Well I guess I shouldn't worry. I'm mobile too, and you're a grown man capable of taking care of yourself!"

"Si querida. You never have to worry about me. You do enough stressing already."

"I don't think I'm actually worried. Just wondering if you'll get bored waiting for me to get back." She continued to chew on the pencil.

"I promise to always occupy myself when you are

working. Even though you should know it pleases me to think about watching you create these amazing travel adventures on the ground. I admire the tenacity and grit it takes to be self-employed!"

"Thank you!" She blushed, proud of what she had accomplished.

"I know it takes something to branch out on one's own. I created a successful management consulting business after university."

"What happened with that?" She asked curious.

"I sold it. My family asked that I come and support them instead."

"Was that disappointing?" Mira inquired.

"Not at all. I proved to myself I could do it. I didn't have to rely on my family indefinitely. I could be independent and pay them back."

"They must have been very proud?"

"I think so. We never really talked about it. Tia Catherine was more concerned with me settling down and having a family."

"You were too young for that!"

"Ha! Tia Catherine is always conspiring to set us up. Even after Mama's passing, Tia has never forgotten the dream she and my mother had to keep up the pressure until all of us were settled.”

“What about your father?”

“Papa didn’t offer his opinion when we were young. He simply said he knew his sons would make their own way in the world.”

“And now that you are grown and older?”

“He wants us to find a love like he had with Mama.”

“My parents offer me advice all the time. Perhaps too much advice at times. Don’t get me wrong. I’m grateful and sometimes it’s too much!”

“Well, your business is unique and intriguing. I promise not to offer advice unless requested. Consider me a fan, quietly looming in the background!”

“Deal! And I’ll definitely make time for meals, and maybe even you can experiment with me sometimes. I like getting your feedback; a male’s perspective.”

“You might have noticed I only offer advice if you insist. Otherwise, I keep my opinion to myself.”

He leaned in and lowered his voice. “I hope we’ll have time to make love on every trip. That could make for good research too, si?”

She closed her eyes briefly, not wanting to imagine all the pent up passion that idea evoked. Yet, she couldn't help imagining them in exotic locales.

"Oh I already can see your mind working!"

She balled up the piece of paper she'd been doodling on, and threw it across the desk. "You are incorrigible!" she proclaimed trying to keep a straight face.

He swatted it away, as he got up from the chair. Like a tiger on the prowl, he went to the door, and turned the lock, then he covered the few feet to be at her side. He leaned over to whisper in her ear.

"You know we could start practicing now?"

"Practicing what?" She said turning slightly in her chair slowly towards him.

He leaned in to touch his head to her ear once again, this time trapping her with his hands holding both arms of her office chair.

"Me providing a male's perspective on making love to the most beautiful woman I've ever seen, right here, right now!"

"Wait, what? I thought you said we were not making love…" Her head was foggy with lust. He smelled so damn good with the mix of lemon and woodsy scent. *That cologne…*

"Shhhh, it's not tonight yet." He said as he knelt down in front of her. "I will show you a new experience," was the last thing she heard as he slid her chair towards his muscled body, parting her legs. She was fascinated, intrigued and immediately lost in his expert touch. She was sure they were about to have the most pleasurable, unforgettable experience. *Damn, being in her office would never be the same again!*

As he placed his lips on her inner left thigh, all she could do was succumb…

Chapter 29

"Without communication, there is no relationship. Without respect, there is no love. Without trust, there is no reason to continue." ~ Author Unknown

St. Augustine, FL

Xavier knocked on the door to her house. As soon as the plane landed back from New York, he gave his father a quick tour of the new house and drove to see her. Every day away from his Mira seemed like an eternity. He couldn't wait to kiss her, hold her in his arms. Maybe if he was lucky they'd end up in bed. It was a Saturday after all.

"What are you doing here Xavier?" Her mood seemed different, almost defensive.

"Remember, I said I'd come by when I got back?"

"Yeah, whatever. Now is not a good time…"

"What's wrong Mira? Tell me?"

Just at that moment a neighbor walked by. "Morning Mira, everything good?"

He watched as she leaned around him and waved to the man. "Yes Sam, I'm good!"

"Who is that?"

She turned her attention back to Xavier. "That's my neighbor. Don't act jealous. I don't want a scene on my front doorstep, so I'm going to briefly let you in." She turned her back on him, and walked away from the door.

Xavier felt like he'd been punched in the stomach. He wasn't sure what was going on and he was going to get to the bottom of it. She continued walking to the back of the house towards the kitchen. He stepped inside, closed the door and followed her.

"Sit down Xavier," she said pointing to the kitchen table where they'd had many meals.

He sat, patiently waiting to hear what was wrong.

"I'm so angry with you!"

"Why? I have no idea what you're talking about."

She turned to the kitchen counter and picked up some scattered printed papers and threw them across the table at him. "I gave you my trust, my heart, and my body. And you're playing me for the fool. Is this what you were doing in New York? Or should I say who you were doing?"

He looked down at the article on the first page in the trash magazine. *"Off the Market?"* The photo was grainy, but it looked to be the front of his condo building in New York City. A woman was coming out of the glass doors, and Xavier assumed what he was seeing was a picture of Dana leaving his place months ago. The print date three days prior. The photo had the subtext: *"Things look to be heating up for Playboy Xavier Gutiérrez and his on again off again love interest, Dana Stratton.*" He knew she hadn't been back to his place unless she was visiting another resident in the building. He exhaled. The damn tabloids keep causing issues. He looked up into the face of disgust.

"Mira, this garbage paper spews lies. You're misinterpreting."

"Am I?" She said putting her hands on her hips. "Is that not your place? The woman called Dana you were in a relationship with? You know the one you told me about. I looked her up. This is her!" She said pointing to the photo.

"Mira, I haven't seen her in months. I wouldn't lie to you!"

"Unless you were caught red-handed? You can't have us both!" She said in a raised voice, just below a yell.

"Mira, Mira calm down!" He said in an even tone which he hoped would have her actually calm down.

"Don't tell me to calm down! You can get out! I don't know why I listened to you in the first place. I knew you were trouble!"

"Please come sit down," he said patting the seat next to him. "Talk to me, not accuse me! I don't lie. Not to you, not to anyone." He hoped his continued calmness would prevail and get her to recognize her sense of logic. And he prayed she would let him explain before she decided to make him get out.

He watched her shift from foot to foot. He had gotten through to her. She pushed out a breath, and went to sit in the farthest chair from him. He suppressed a smile. She was a very logically minded woman, rationale and someone who doesn't jump to unfounded conclusions. He had no worries he could prove to her the story was manufactured.

"Fine! Start talking, Xavier!"

"Thank you, Mira, for listening to me. Before you ever agreed to go out on a date with me, I was back in New York for business meetings. I believe this was right after I selected the new house. When I walked into my apartment, Dana was there. She had a key to my place and I had forgotten to retrieve it when we split. She wanted to get back together and I said no. I walked out five minutes later and told her to get out, leave my key and have a nice life! I had the locks changed and instructed management to not ever let her in again. This picture, I assume, was from that day. That's the whole story. I swear on my Mama's grave!"

"Why should I believe you?"

"What do I gain from lying? All I've told you is easily verifiable."

"You have enough money to fix the truth!"

"Mira, you are being unreasonable! You already know that the paparazzi hawk my family looking for reasons to spin the truth to sell papers. We've had similar conversations in the past. I can't do anything about them hiding in the shadows to portray us in salacious stories. I live as you've seen: work, family, you!"

"I'm being unreasonable because I don't like surprises. I was trusting you. Now I don't know."

"Mira, why would I want her if I have you. You are intelligent, beautiful, adventurous, fun, mostly undramatic! Even if I didn't have you, I still wouldn't want her."

"Wait, did you just call me dramatic?"

He laughed. "Mira, Mira…this is drama! If you want to know anything of me, just ask. I have nothing to hide. I have never even hidden my feelings from you."

She exhaled. "Okay, maybe I was misguided by that article. And a little irrational. Maybe a touch dramatic."

He reached his hand across the table. "Mira give me your hand?" He watched as she begrudgingly put her hand in his.

"Everything can be worked out in communication. I'm here because I want to be with you. I'm with you. I love you, and I don't want anyone outside of us to come between us. Promise you will bring it to me, whatever it is and we will work through it together?” He rubbed her hand trying to show her he was sensitive to her feelings.

She briefly closed her eyes. “Okay that’s fair. I can do that.” She sighed.

“Thank you! I do appreciate you showing me this, so I can let our lawyers deal with it. I was stupid to not get my keys back long ago. I only have eyes for you. I would never have minded if it were you leaving my place that the paparazzi photographed.”

“I was ready to murder you last night when I saw this!” She said pointing to the paper.

“How do we call a truce?”

“You’ve explained what happened and I believe you.” She said putting her hands up in surrender.

“Maybe now I can have my welcome back kiss?”

“I suppose that could be arranged.” He watched as she arose from the chair and came over to give him a peck on the cheek.

“That’s it? After your yelling, and making me sit? I even had to endure your neighbor, Sam’s glares!”

“Well, what did you have in mind?” She giggled.

"Definitely this," he said scooping her from standing to sitting across his lap. He leaned down to kiss her, leaving no one to mistake or wonder if he was into her or not. She had become his heartbeat, the source of his contentment. He needed her to be okay with the unintentional impacts of loving him.

"Happy now?" She asked him.

"I'm getting there. That kiss was a good start!"

Mira pulled her shirt over her head and released her bra.

"How about now?"

"Oh, this is turning into a better morning," he said as he cupped her breasts. She moaned and wiggled on his lap. He was rock hard now, and would not be satisfied until he was buried inside of her. He stood up, pushed the papers to the floor and placed her on the kitchen table. He kissed her as he gently spread her legs with his hands, so he could place his body between them. He was apologetic about the article, and not sorry it ended them up here. He and Mira were amazing together, and they were about to feel amazing together.

"What are you doing, Xavier? How did we get here?"

"I'm about to bring you immense pleasure. Do you want to be pleased?" He drew circles over her breasts, and ran his finger down her chest to the center of her core. He slid his hand under her minidress and inside her panties. She was already wet, as if she was waiting for him.

"Oh yes. I absolutely want…" With her pronouncement he could not think anymore. All he wanted was to feel her. Hot, wet and moaning his name on her hips. And so it shall be…

Chapter 30

"Time together as a family is a gift."
~ Joanna Gaines

The Next Day...

Xavier invited Mira to the new home he had refreshed for his father. Yesterday, after he'd explained to her that she'd jumped to conclusions and they'd made love, he nonchalantly mentioned he'd brought his Papa back to Florida to the new house. He asked that she come over today in the early afternoon to meet the man he'd rearranged so much of his life to please. Mira had been excited to oblige.

She rang the doorbell, and waited no more than thirty seconds before the door opened.

"Buenos Dias Mira, Mira," he said as he stepped aside so she could walk into the house. He greeted her with a hug and kiss once the door was closed.

"Hello to you too!" She said when he stopped kissing her.

"If my Papa was not here, I would scoop you up and take you to bed," he quietly spoke in her ear.

"Yes well, thank goodness for small blessings! I am excited to meet your father, not entertain you!"

"Point noted, at least for now. This way Mira," he said. He walked her into the living room on the right side of the house. Sitting in front of a futbol game on the big screen television, was the man she knew had to be his father.

"Papa! Mira's here!"

His father, pressed the mute button on the television, and got to his feet. Mira was taken aback at the sight of a man who looked to be the spitting image of Xavier, with the exception of his salt and pepper colored hair. Similar height at six feet, and with beautiful olive skin that was a birthright of their Spanish heritage.

"Mira this is my Papa!" Xavier said approaching his father.

She walked close and stopped next to Xavier. "It is nice to meet you Senor Gutiérrez," she said offering a hand to shake.

"Ah Mira! Please call me Macario," he said in a thick accent as he offered his hand in greeting to politely shake. "You are the woman who has tamed my bambino! You not only are a beauty, I know you must also possess great patience."

"Papa, let's not have Mira thinking there is something about me that requires patience."

"I would never say such things in polite company!" To that comment Mira laughed out loud.

"I am fully aware of your son's need to control everything. Sometimes I let him win and we won't tell him," she said as she winked at Senor Gutiérrez.

"I can't believe the two of you are talking as if I was not here."

"Xavier, your father and I are comparing notes. I think it is most appropriate!"

"Don't make me regret having you two meet!"

"Tranquilo, Xavier!" Which meant no big deal in Spanish slang. Mira appreciated the ease in which the men interacted.

"Right, Xavier! There is no harm to our chatter. Be worried if we start whispering."

"I like her, Xa!" His father said looking at his son.

"Me too Papa. Now let's go eat. I had lunch delivered."

"Works for me. Then you can tell me all about life in New York." Mira asked.

"My pleasure to fill you in."

The rest of the afternoon was pleasant, and Mira really liked Senor Gutiérrez too. She wasn't quite able to call him by his first name. That seemed disrespectful. He extended an invitation for her to visit Jaen. He and Xavier also discussed something called the '*Spring Festival*.' Mira knew nothing about it. After much laughter, food and futbol talk while they finished watching sports, Mira thought it a good time to go.

"Thank you both for a lovely afternoon. I really must be going though."

"I wish you would stay." Xavier added.

"I'm sorry to say, I have some calls to return." Xavier knew Mira was being polite in order to give him and Papa some time to settle into the new house, at least for now. Xavier had told her he wasn't sure if Papa would stay more than a few days.

"Mira, remember what I said? Whatever you need. If my son does not conform, just call me and I will ensure he will!"

"I feel like you two are now actively conspiring against me!" Xavier said in a feigned frown.

"You've been warned, mi hijo! Mira is in good hands."

 "Mira, let me walk you out."

All Mira could do was laugh. "This was such a fun time! I will look forward to our next meeting. Might I give you a hug, Senor?"

"Of course." Xavier watched as his Papa stood up, and Mira put her arms around the man he loved more than life. She gave him a genuine hug. That warmed Xavier's heart. Even with all the banter, he could tell the two of them were great company. Not that he was worried about Mira, and his Papa was another story.

Xavier caught her hand after the hug and walked her to the front door. "Mira, Mira, thank you for being so kind with my Papa!"

"Your father is a jewel, indeed. He was very kind to me and has a great sense of humor. I will look forward to the next time!"

"Me too! And that reminds me. Tia Catherine and Tio Antonio did ask me to bring you to the upcoming *Spring Festival* in Spain. I hope you will say yes. Now that you've met Papa, I want you to meet the rest of the family too. And that event will be lots of fun and fiesta!"

"I'd love to, if my schedule permits. Give me the dates and I will check the calendar. Really, I do want to go. If I'm free, I'll be there. Your family has to be riot to be around, if your brother and father are any indication!"

"You have no idea! I'll send the dates over later. I know you have to be going. Give me a goodbye kiss?"

"I suppose I could conform to that." No sooner than she got the words out of her mouth did he pull her into his arms and kiss her breathless.

"Until later…I'll see if I can sneak out and come spend the night with you." He whispered.

"You will do no such thing! Enjoy your father's company. We have plenty of time to be together." She was tempted to stay, and she needed to go.

"You promise?"

"I do. Buenas tardes Xavier." With that she turned and he opened the door for her. He stood there until she was in her car, and he put his hand up to say goodbye. She waved and backed carefully out of his driveway. After turning the corner, she exhaled, already missing being in his presence. On her drive home, she wondered more about meeting the rest of his family in Spain. Would they be as kind and inviting as Senor Gutiérrez? Would it be fun to see Xavier in his element? With his cousins? Perhaps she would rearrange life to be there…

Chapter 31

"If you want to walk fast, walk alone. If you want to walk far, walk together." ~ African Proverb

Spring Festival - Jaen, Spain

"Bienvenido a casa Xa, le major de todas mis primos!" Translated as welcome home Xa, the best of all my cousins.

Xavier smirked, as he embraced his cousin Alberto, one of the six Gutierrez brothers. He already sensed a smile from his often too serious cousin. Xa was not Alberto's favorite cousin, as there were no favorites in this family. That was one form of greeting they used to joke in front of newcomers. They always said Marcelo is Tia's favorite and she would scold them, by saying: *"You all are equals, and thus, I love all of you equally."*

"Alberto, it's good to see you. Where is Bella? I want to introduce your brilliant, beautiful wife to my equally brilliant and beautiful, Mira."

He'd switched to English for Mira's benefit. Xa knew Mira understood Spanish, and only spoke it when absolutely necessary. She'd shocked him responding to her client in their native tongue. Alberto spoke excellent English based on his scientific role in the company.

"What? Am I not good enough to meet the woman who has tamed you? Everyone wants Bella." His cousin feigned shock.

"Since you're married now and off the market, I have no problem introducing you. Mira, this is my cousin Alberto. The only Gutierrez brother who stayed in Jaen. Watch out for him though, he broods and then we're all in trouble!"

"It is my pleasure to meet you, Mira. Xa is delusional! I'm mild-mannered and unassuming."

"If you say so, Primo."

"It's very nice to meet you, Alberto." He watched as Mira, smiling, offered her hand in greeting.

"Please ignore the banter between us. Actually let me apologize now to you for the antics between all of us! I am the second best behaved of the lot."

"He's exaggerating Mira! We are on our best behavior in public."

"You all are fun. I can already see!"

"Wait till we're all together!" Xavier watched the casual ease will which his cousin was talking about them, and the ease with which Mira seemed to be absorbing it all. Xavier thought it best to steer this conversation away from their antics. He was not trying to scare her away any more than already seen.

"Primo, really, where is Arabella? Is she not coming?"

"Right, I got distracted. Bella's coming later. She's working on some last minute issue in the lab."

"Nothing major to impact the upcoming harvest?"

"No, no. I think she just wanted to ensure I was here by sending me home first."

"That makes sense. Mira, Bella is not only Alberto's wife, she's his boss too! Together they oversee our family's olive oil harvest and production."

"Very impressive that you take orders from a woman!"

"Yes, it didn't start out very pretty, and we worked through it. We went from being at war to falling in love. Now, I gladly submit to her at work and am getting lots of practice at home too! I am a bit spoiled and stubborn my madre says. In spite of it, I'm learning that American saying: *a happy wife means a happy life*!"

They all laughed. Xa knew his cousin's story was one for the history books; no one could have predicted it would turn out so well. Except maybe, wise Tia Catherine, who had a unique sense—as if she was Cupid herself. Xa was falling for Mira and was hopeful for their continued togetherness into the future. Maybe a conversation with Tia would seal his fate to Mira. He'd have to be cautious though

because Tia could be somewhat overbearing. She was
well intentioned, and if she thought Mira worthy, he
would be married by daybreak and working to make
babies. Lots of babies, she wanted, Tia reminded
them at every chance. His relationship with Mira was
still new and they were in no way ready for that.

"Don't you all look amazing!" He knew his aunt's
voice. They turned to see Tio Antonio escorting his
beloved, Tia Catherine.

They all greeted in traditional cheek-to-cheek
Spanish style. Mira fit right in even though she was
meeting them for the first time.

"Tia, how uncanny! I was just thinking of you, and
here you are!" Xa said in a weary tone. The matriarch
of the family watched over her sons and nephews like
a hawk.

"All good thoughts, I hope?"

"Si, as always Tia." He really loved her and most of
the time, he was grateful that she took his brother and
him under her wing after Mama died.

"Excelente! Is this 'the Mira Morales?'"

"Yes, Tia Catherine and Tio Antonio, please meet
Mira. Mira, this is my aunt and uncle, Senor and
Senora Gutiérrez, I have talked so much about. They
were instrumental in raising us to be good men."

“It is a pleasure to officially meet you both. Thank you for such a kind welcome!”

“It is our pleasure to have you this evening! We hope you are finding everything enjoyable.” Tia spoke again.

“Thank you again for your generosity! The gift basket was lovely. I’m happy to be invited!”

“Si, Mira, you are a beauty amongst beauties this evening.” Tio, always a charming host lifted her hand to his lips. “Qué bellísima eres!!”

“Thank you, Senor.”

“Please, drop the Senor. It’s Antonio!” This seemed to be a theme for the older Gutiérrez males.

“Of course, Sir.”

“Mama,” he said turning to his wife, “You see they always remind us of our age.”

Tia smiled meeting her husband’s gaze with wisdom in her eyes. “Oh dear Mira, please indulge my husband and his legendary, harmless charm. He is trying to recapture his youth.”

They all laughed once more.

“You all are just the cutest couple!” Mira spoke aloud.

"Please Mira, don't encourage them!" Alberto requested. "They can be unbearable, like two teenagers who just fell for each other!"

"How do you think you all came about?" Tio said.

"See! Yuck!" Alberto threw his hands in the air as if to prove his point.

"Alberto, you are lucky. Your parents are young and spry. And they know how to throw a great party. I love this theme!"

Xa listened to the engaging small talk. Mira was confident, polite, and unafraid of a challenge. He admired her for moving across the world with purpose, and yet she was so real with people. It was her gift.

"Thank you, dear for saying that." Tia continued. "We do a carnival for three days, and the last day in the evening, tonight, we host a themed party as a fundraiser for less fortunate families in this region of Espana. This time, the children at the lower school came up with '*A Spring Fling*.' We said okay, let's go with it! The whole of Jaen is invited to the *Spring Fling Carnival* with free food, games and rides. This dance event is open to them and donors alike so everyone can see we are one world of all peoples who help one another. Businesses from all over provide services like free hairdressing, barbering, pampering and daycare. And there is a clothing bazaar that happens weeks ahead so that everyone has something to wear. Most of the children prefer the town's theater sponsored movie marathon tonight in lieu of coming to this stuffy dance!"

"What a great contribution! I'm sorry to have missed the carnival. I was preparing a job in nearby Italy. Tonight though is spectacular with ice sculptures, chocolate fountains, an olive bar and this delicious champagne!" Mira held up her glass. "I am sure the carnival was just as magical with pure, childhood fun!"

"There's always next year, same timeframe so you can plan ahead. That is unless my dear nephew messes up your relationship."

He put his arm around Mira's waist. "My beloved Tia, I promise I will bring Mira to carnival next year. You have my word."

"You better! Mira is stunning, and looks perfectly suited on your arm."

"Thank you for the invitation. I would like to come again." Mira sounded non-committal, even though he felt her body leaning into his embrace.

"What else have you two been up to?" Tia tilted her head. He suspected she wanted to know the exact nature of his relationship with Mira. She was inquisitive for sure with laser cut precision. Yet, she wouldn't dare interrogate him unmercifully in front of company. He could offer scant details.

"Mira and I went to the Caribbean. One of the U.S. Virgin Islands, St. Thomas. It is a little far from Espana. It is a place where one is able to lay back and unwind for a few days."

"How close is it from where you now are in Florida?"

"Maybe a couple hours flight," he said nonchalantly.

"That's close."

"If any of you ever come visit me and Papa when we're in America, we can definitely take you to check it out. I see why Javier and Olivia are settled in the Caribbean Sea—beautiful water mixed with turquoise, sapphire and aqua green hues. If my Papa ever decides to give up socializing with his newly found East Coast friends, perhaps I will buy Mira an island in that sea."

"Perhaps one Gutierrez family is enough there!" Xavier knew what Tia wasn't saying; she hated how far away Javier and Olivia lived from Spain. Being in other locales for their business was a necessary evil; if one choose to leave the family business, Tia felt they could live on the European continent and be close to Jaen.

Mira shook her head. "No thank you, Xavier," she said smiling. "An island is probably too remote for me."

"You liked St. Thomas, si?" He asked.

"That was different. Even though we didn't partake of all St. Thomas has to offer, it's not desolated like what you describe of Javier's island. It has a bustling industry, restaurants, spas, and thousands of people!"

"Very true. There are lots of established places to go on island." He looked to the rest of the group, still noticing Tia's intense interest.

"What did you all do there?"

Xavier was determined to not cave to Tia's investigative prowess.

"We relaxed mostly. One night, we ate at a restaurant that was a renovated stone farmhouse."

"I love farmhouses," Tia said tapping her fingers together. "Tell me more about it?"

Mira spoke up first, and he loved the grace she displayed mixing and mingling with his familia.

"That is an elegant place. *The Stone Farmhouse*, I think it's called. A quaint and romantic location on the north end of the island near the famous Magen's Bay. It has indoor and outdoor seating, stone steps with multicolored masonry and there was a courtyard too. The entry and doorways all displayed circular symmetry. White coverings, fine china and silverware over wooden tables framed against stone walls that hold rustic looking sconces. Even though the restaurant is not on the water, it is an idyllic setting for a wedding, a sunset rendezvous, or party such as this." Her capture of detail impressed him.

"It sounds phenomenal! How was the food?" He was sure Tia could have cared less about their meal.

"Divine, actually. I was skeptical that everything could come together in such a setting. They have a French inspired menu. They bake baguettes of bread and whip their own butter too!"

"How could you go wrong with whipped butter!" Everyone laughed.

"You travel the world Mira! How does St. Thomas compare?" Tio asked.

"It is in my top twenty. Pretty water, lots of mountainous terrain, good shopping, and friendly people. It was a perfect getaway for a few days of rest and relaxation. I appreciate Xavier's kidnapping me because I needed all those treats!" She turned away from his possessive hold to stand on her own, and she looked into his eyes.

"Perhaps we should make a point of going to visit these U.S. islands, Papa," Tia said.

"I keep telling Xavier, I am so grateful and much nicer to my clients as a result."

Xavier nodded in agreement, not daring to interrupt her. St. Thomas forever would hold a special magic for him and he loved their *Buoy Haus, Frenchman's Reef Cove*.

He swore he could see pinkness rising in her cheeks as no doubt she too was reminiscing about their frolicking and escapades on the beach. What he wouldn't give to be back there now at that resort. It would be just the two of them making love on their patio's swing wrapped in a blanket once more as they did that rainy afternoon. Pouring rain and not a soul who was willing to venture past and get drenched. The ultimate intimacy and privacy any couple could ask for. He'd make sure they went back there again and again to capture the magic of their first time.

"Wait! What? Is that Lea? Why is she with TM?" Cousin Alberto interrupted his thoughts of their trip to St. Thomas.

Tia Catherine was first to register Alberto's words, and turned away from their previously engrossing conversation. Tio, Mira and Xavier followed suit to look across the ballroom.

"My word! It is indeed Lea with my wayward son!" Tia said.

"You weren't aware they were coming?" Alberto looked to his mother. If anyone was to know, it would be Tia Catherine.

"Not at all my dear. All Tomas had told me is he was bringing a plus one. I stopped asking long ago who it would be." She looked at them and they knew she spoke truth.

"Well this is a shocker!" Tio Antonio noted.

Tia turned back to her husband. "I'd almost given up hope of our youngest child ever doing anything appropriate. Lea, she is family."

"Mama, let's not count our chickens before they hatch," Alberto chimed in.

Everyone seemed quite amused, except Xavier who suspected his cousin, and closest friend on the planet, was up to something. It was not like TM to not mention he'd made contact again with Lea, their childhood playmate.

"Oh no doubt they've hatched as a couple," Tia said with confidence. "Bringing Lea here to the *Spring Fling Dance* is a statement to all of us. They're together!"

"How can you be sure?" Mira asked innocently. Xavier was sure she was making polite conversation in the midst of a drama she didn't know existed.

"I know my son, my dear. While he can act like a jackass when he's out partying, Lea means too much to our family. He would never toy with her."

"Papa, nothing to say?" Alberto asked.

"Mama's said it all." Tio's lips were pursed. Rarely had Xavier seen concern on his uncle's face.

"I just hope Lea knows what she's gotten herself into." Alberto noted.

Tia countered. "I think it's TM who needs to watch out. Lea has always been very decisive and knows her own mind."

"Good point, Mama!" Alberto agreed.

"If you all will excuse us. Papa, please escort me over to greet the happy pair?"

"Of course, my bride!"

They all watched as the couple gracefully moved across the room.

"I'd love to be a fly on the wall observing that conversation." Alberto said.

"I wouldn't." Xavier said drily.

"What do you know Xa?"

"Nothing, and that's what concerns me!"

"You don't think it's just a ruse to get my parents off his back so they'll set him free of their watch. It wouldn't be unusual for TM."

"No, I don't. Lea is like a sister to us. Yet he holds her hand in a way that says 'she's mine!'"

"Oh you're right! This is not good!" Alberto agreed.

"Are you two okay? You don't seem happy for TM. From what Xavier has said of his wild ways, surely his appearance with Lea is good, right?"

"Maybe. And maybe not!" Alberto said. "If you two will excuse me, this is too much! I'm going to go inquire of my wife. Again Mira, a pleasure to meet you. When I find Bella, I will bring her to meet you." Alberto bowed slightly and disappeared into the crowd.

Xavier didn't want to think about TM or try to resolve anything for his grown cousin. It was too much, as Alberto had said. He couldn't believe Lea would accept TM as a mate with all his misadventures. They were nothing alike. Tia would get to the bottom of it and he'd address his cousin's secret later…much later. He turned to the breathtakingly beautiful woman standing before him.

"Ah Mira, Mira. I have been rude. Enough of our family drama. The night is young. Come dance with me?"

"If you insist." She seemed not to care how abruptly he'd dropped the TM and Lea subject. He now was the one who was grateful.

He pulled her by the hand in the opposite direction of TM and Lea, determined to have a great night—one in which he hoped ended up in more love making with Mira.

****

The next morning, Tia invited everyone over to the palazzo for brunch. Xavier excused himself from the social time, and went off in search of his cousin, TM. He was sure Mira could carry her own, and he needed to find out what was going on. Xavier suspected he'd find TM hiding out in the library.

"You know you could have told me!" Xavier said interrupting his cousin's television time as he walked through the library door.

"Told you what?" His cousin feigned ignorance.

"You know what!" Xavier spoke in a stern voice to let his cousin know he was not playing.

"About me and Lea, yeah. You know I couldn't."

"I have been on your side all this time, taking the heat for you. Saving your ass with Tio and Tia."

"I appreciate everything you've done to get me on the right track!"

"This is a right track?"

"Really, Xa. It was better you didn't know. Then you didn't have to lie to the parents."

"You are the one who made a grand entrance last night!"

"Yeah that was awkward, but necessary!" TM shrugged his shoulder as if it was no big deal.

"Of all the women in the world, Lea, really? We grew up with her. She's like our sister!"

"Not to me. Not anymore!"

"How long has this been going on with you two?"

"Can I be honest with you?"

"Oh, now you want to be honest?" Xavier put his arms up in exasperation.

"It's time. We've resisted our attraction to each other long enough. We've worried about what everyone would think. It was no use for me. No matter what party I went to or event, I could only think of her. It was time to face our families."

"Don't break her heart!"

"I won't!"

"You say that TM! I know you! You change women like you change your undergarments."

"It's different this time. I won't ever hurt Lea. Not only do I not want to, I know there would be hell to pay with all of you if I did. I only act like a moron when I'm not with her."

"She's been good with all your publicity and antics?"

"I wouldn't necessarily say she was good with it. But she understood that I was having fun before we reconnected. And then when she would break it off with me, I would spiral and try to forget her."

"How much of this does Tia know?"

"As little as possible from me. You know Mama, she knows more than she ever tells."

"Has she confronted you yet?"

"No. I know it's just a matter of time. It's like she wants me to confess or something. She's so consumed with having us settle down and make babies! I haven't thought that far yet. Just getting Lea to come with me to the dance was hard enough!"

"I really don't know what to say to you. I know with Mira, I am not myself. I will do anything for her and to keep her in my life."

"I think that means you're in love with her."

"I know I'm in love with Mira. Are you in love with Lea?"

"I might be. We are exploring our feelings."

"I don't like any of this! Just be sure. I repeat, do not break her heart. Best friend and blood or not TM, I will beat the hell out of you!"

"I get it. Lea and I will figure this out. Thanks for coming to find me. I didn't want to lie to you."

"Well from now on, how about you just be straight. I am tired of covering for you. The hawking paparazzi don't seem to respect our privacy. And I will not do any more party saves for you. It will come between Mira and me. I will not jeopardize our relationship anymore, even for you.

"You are in love! That's a beautiful thing. Wait till I tell the brothers. You're a marked man."

"You are the butt of the jokes this week. Not me…I gotta get back to the brunch. I can't leave Mira alone to be cornered by your mother." They both laughed, knowing those were wise words. Xavier gave TM a man hug, and then headed back to the front of the house.

Chapter 32

"I will never stop trying. Because when you find the one...you never give up." ~ Crazy, Stupid, Love

Florida

"We need to talk. "

"Wait. Men don't ask to talk!"

"Mira please. Stop stereotyping me!"

"Okay, fine. Meet me here at my place tonight. I'm available any time after five. "

"No, we need a neutral place. Not mine or yours."

"Any ideas what might qualify as neutral?"

"You tell me?"

"Let's take a walk. Meet me at *Jax Beach Fishing Pier*, five thirty so we can both account for traffic!"

"I'll be there. Thank you for being willing."

"Okay," she sighed. He was the consummate gentleman. Polite. Always asking her opinion, never boastful or bragging.

"It's okay Mira. No one's dying because we are choosing to have a conversation."

"Will you stop saying no one's dying? We all die a little bit more each day. I'm not the one being significant about this. You are the one who wants to discuss your agenda."

"Si. I just want to talk, querida."

"Five thirty, *Jax Beach Pier*. I have to go!"

She pushed the disconnect button on her home office phone. Enough already! She liked that he called her "dear" in his native tongue. And she hated it too as she felt like she was being sucked into his honey trap. She turned in her home office chair to stare out at the garden. Floor to ceiling windows and sliding glass doors were purposefully installed to give Mira the feeling of being one with nature on the other side of those panes. Florida summers were hot, starting their temperature climb in the early hours of the day. From her office, she could have temperature control and beauty all at the same time. Everything was always in bloom with year round warmer temperatures. Pink pentas, which grew nonstop were mixed in with lavender—her favorite two flowers as both were irresistible to hummingbirds and butterflies. At the corner edge of the yard, a man-made babbling brook, that the gardener called a water stream, using recycled water from the rain run-off. It gave an illusion of naturally occurring from the downward slope that the gravel, rocks and small waterfall produced. If one was outside, they could hear the run of the water produced by water aerator and quality management system. This by far was one of the best scenes. It went a long way to calm her nerves when life was not going according to her plans. Being self-employed, she controlled her own narrative, made her own rules, and that was the way she liked it.

Xavier's demand foretold of a conversation she didn't plan to ever have. She was sure this "talk' was about their relationship. Still tenuous and yet intense. He'd been asking her for weeks to express her feelings for him. And she'd been resisting. He was such a distraction to her. She supposed he was a good distraction, and she didn't like that she enjoyed his company just a bit too much. St. Thomas had been a mistake. She'd never meant to sleep with him—a momentary slip of her façade that kept happening. Her armor was back up. Well not really. She knew she didn't need a companion, nor did she need distractions. He was distracting. She had even been imagining what it would be like to have him travel with her all the time. She shook her head. *Men don't follow women around the world! Snap out of your fantasy and get back to work. Get it done and move on to the next task.* Later today was yet to be lived. Mira appreciated she was practical, focused and didn't spend much time fantasizing. That was, until she met Xavier. She sighed and turned back to her laptop, leaving nature and all its beauty behind.

****

Jax Beach Pier

"Hello Xavier."

"Hello querida." He held open his arms, and she

stepped into them as he placed the customary kisses on both her cheeks. Spanish kisses she'd labeled them since they'd met. She suspected he was purposefully avoiding any public displays of affection. Media could be lurking. He was a fast learner, that's for sure….

"Let's walk the pier? It makes for good exercise."

"As you wish." He said gesturing towards the ramp that would take them up the pier to the entrance desk.

She started walking on leaden legs, wishing the ground would open up and swallow her whole. Then she wouldn't have to "talk."

Xavier made payment and she led the way, walking down the center so as not to get caught in any fishers' lines. There was very little rail space even so late in the day. *Jax Beach Pier*, a quarter mile long out into the Atlantic Ocean is a central place to catch fish for both amateurs and professionals, weather-permitting. Open from six in the morning until eleven at night, there were lots of comings and goings and plenty of invisible lines attached to fishing poles—everyone hopeful the fish were biting in the shallow waters below. Some of the day's catch would end up on the plates prepared by local chefs and others would go to homes perhaps to be eaten tonight or frozen for another day. In the companionable silence that they had fallen into, she looked around. She could wait him out. This was his plan, his agenda and he'd control their interaction even in this "neutral place," where the ocean breezes and crashing waves against the shore set the stage of their unspoken power struggle. The wind was always blowing here even on the warmest days.

"There are moments Mira when we could be best friends. And others where I feel like we are strangers. Why must you keep pushing me away?"

"It's a beautiful day out here." His comments caught her off guard, interrupting her visual musings of the myriad of sites.

"It is! You aren't answering my question. Why Mira?"

"What you said was a statement. You're convinced you're right. You're also convinced your charms will work on me."

"That's not fair!"

"I'm not an international model, Xavier. I'm not Lella who is living life in the spotlight for paparazzi to snap photos at every turn. Nor am I some woman who wants to get caught up."

"I've explained that life is not me. Should I have to lose what we have for the sake of helping my cousins stay out of trouble?"

"No, I didn't say that!"

"You're not saying much."

"There isn't much to say. You know I'm not comfortable with this. With an us. Even if I want an us, it doesn't make it comfortable,"

"You see that?" He said pointing to the fisherman who had just set a baby shark on his cutting board. "Even the sharks eventually get caught."

"Is that your plan? To catch me, gut me and then take the parts you like to throw the rest aside!'"

He stopped walking, and pulled her into his arms. "No, that is not my intention at all."

"What then is your intention?"

"My intention is to love you, right this minute, even in my frustration, and your denial of our chemistry!"

Before she could respond, he kissed her. Right there on *Jax Beach Pier*. When his lips touched hers, it ignited a fire just like that afternoon in St. Thomas on that patio. All the life around them ceased to exist. No one and nothing but Mira and Xavier—only this moment mattered. She put her arms around his neck and leaned into him. She couldn't argue, she simply stopped resisting. If he hadn't been holding her in his arms, she'd have fallen from the pent up passion. This man, this moment. All too soon, he stopped and broke away from her.

"Let's go. Here is not the place for this, and we will finish what we started." She nodded no doubt they would finish this—she had to, just as if it was as critical as her next breath. He took her hand and led her back the way they came.

He'd won this round. Hell, he was winning every round. And she was okay with it…

Chapter 33

"And now here is my secret, a very simple secret: It is only with the heart that one can see rightly; what is essential is invisible to the eye."
~ Antoine de Saint-Exupéry, The Little Prince

Ponte Vedra, FL

Mira was fidgeting back and forth as she waited for Xavier to arrive. She was sitting on the sofa, flipping through the pages of some home magazine her mother had on the end table. Today was the day she would introduce him to her parents, Marc and Susana. She'd decided they should meet on a Sunday, as Mira would already be at her parents' house. Afternoon tea, she'd suggested to her mother. That way her mother couldn't interrogate Xavier too much, and she could breathe. Xavier once told her he was good at tea, because Tia Catherine had taught all the boys how to act in polite company. Mira's mom would eat that up. Not that Mira felt that she needed her parents to like Xavier. Even if they didn't, they were kind enough not to say it in front of company. Tea for a couple hours. Then she'd stay for dinner and listen to whatever commentary there was to share.

Promptly at five minutes before two in the afternoon, the doorbell rang. Mira smiled as she went to the door suspecting Xavier had been nearby way before the time they'd agreed upon because he was always early. As she approached the door, she could hear her parents coming to the entry hall to do proper greetings there. She exhaled and pulled the door open.

Standing before her was a gorgeous man, dressed in slacks, a collared shirt and sweater. She told him to absolutely not overdress to meet her parents. And not to kiss her when she opened the door, unless she was alone.

"Hello Mira, Mira."

"Hi Xavier. Please come in."

"Mom, Dad, I'd like you to meet Xavier Gutiérrez."

"Good Afternoon, Mr. and Mrs. Morales. It is very nice to meet you both." Mira knew that Xavier was purposefully using English without his Spanish mixed in.

Mira watched as her mother stepped forward with open arms. "Xavier it is nice to meet you. I'm a hugger, so save the handshake for my husband." Xavier stepped into the welcoming embrace. Mira had given him a heads up that her mother was sometimes over the top, not that Mira had much experience bringing her male friends home to meet her parents.

"Xavier, a pleasure. Call me Marc," her dad said with his more laid back handshake.

"Come, let's go into the living room. Papa and I will then go and get the tea service."

"Would you like some assistance?" Xavier offered.

"Absolutely not. You are a guest in our home.
Please sit. Mira, you choose where." And with that
her parents escaped out of the room.

Once they were out of earshot, Mira showed Xavier
to the loveseat across from the sofa. There was a
coffee table between the two pieces of furniture
where her mom had begun to set up for teatime.

"Mira, Mira. Your parents seem good with meeting
me." He said sitting down.

"Yeah, they're pretty cool! Let me say thank you in
advance for not falling prey to whatever questions
they will have."

"I'm an open book."

He patted to the space next to him for her to come sit.
She complied sitting down while leaving a few
inches between them. He leaned over and whispered
into her ear, "anything they ask, I will answer."

"Stop! Let's not have true confessions, okay?" She
replied back in a hushed tone. He laughed heartily at
that. Mira was serious. Perhaps she should have
worried more about this little meet and greet. She'd
told both her parents to be on their best behavior.

"I'm so glad you've made yourself comfortable,"
Mira's mom said as she came into the room, followed

by dad who carried the silver tray full of the fete of the hour.

"You have a very lovely home. Have you lived in this area of Florida for long?"

"Thank you, Xavier. We like it here. We moved to Florida before Mira was born. We came from New York originally." Mira watched this exchange as if she were a fly on the wall. Her mother poured the tea in fine china, and handed each of them a teacup.

"My wife wanted a warmer existence. It was a great place to raise a child with good schools. So while we could have moved around, we chose to stay in the area. And we love it here as we age."

"My Papa and I have been living mostly in New York for a couple years. I hope that he will come to love it here too. He loves the sea."

"What about your mother?"

"She died when I was a small child."

"I'm sorry. That must have been very traumatic for you."

"Not really. I was only four. I think it was much harder on my Papa and my brother. We have a big family that helped get us through."

"That is a blessing. You have a brother?"

"Yes, Matias. He is four years older than me."

"Does he live in America too?"

"Not very much. He has a few places. He enjoys Monte Carlo most of the time."

"Oh, Monte Carlo. I have always wanted to go there."

"Monaco is beautiful, with many views of the Mediterranean from its cliffs. Monte Carlo seems to hold the most international flare."

"Perhaps someday I will go."

"Do let me know. I am sure I could arrange a tour for you."

"You sound like Mira."

"I don't have the same high level of skill that she does in catering to the needs of others."

"Yes, our daughter is quite the adventure arranger."

"Hi! I'm right here…remember!" Mira waved as a warning to her mother to change the subject. She could feel Xavier watching her.

"Mira tells us you've bought a new home on the ocean." Thankfully her mother got the clue. Mira practiced her slow breathing.

"Yes, ma'am. It is lovely. Mira helped me find it, so I am very grateful! As my father ages, he seems to do better in warmer climates."

"Yes, I too appreciate the warmer climates," her mother agreed.

The niceties continued for the entire time. At some point her dad and Xavier began talking about soccer. Talking sports was a relief to Mira who was concerned her mother wanted more details about Xavier's home life.

"While I am having a lovely time, it is getting late and I should be going." Xavier said.

"Mira did tell us you had evening plans. Well, I've enjoyed our visit with you, and look forward to the next time. Perhaps a Sunday dinner one day soon. And if your father is in town, bring him along too." Mira's mother, the consummate hostess, offered.

"I'd like that very much, Mrs. Morales!"

"Xavier, perhaps one day we can watch a futbol game together. You can explain more of it to me." Her dad said. Mira loved her dad. Always he lightened the mood.

"Absolutely, sir." Xavier agreed.

Everyone rose, and her parents excused themselves. Mira walked Xavier to the door.

"How did I do?"

"Very well!"

"May I have a kiss goodbye?"

"I suppose you earned it!" No sooner than Mira had said that did Xavier pull her into his arms, and kiss her. Nothing too risqué.

"Call me later?"

"Yes, I just need to make it through dinner. You're lucky you get to go!"

"Oh Mira, your parents are well meaning. I love you! No worries." He smiled.

"Love you back!"

Mira let Xavier out and went to sit back down on the couch.

****

"Don't mess this up with your young man!" Mira's mom said upon returning to the living room with her dad at her side.

"Really Mom?" Mira said as she watched her dad sit down on the sofa and pick up the newspaper.

"Yes really!" Her mom said as she started to clean up the tea service. Mira chose to let her mom respond before she said more.

"What your mother is trying to convey is you don't have to bring your past into this relationship with Xavier. You have a blank slate and perhaps you'll settle down." Her dad had decided to chime in.

"I'm not sure where this is going?"

"Exactly the point!" Her mother said staring at her as she sat down on the sofa.

"What your mother is trying to say is we've noticed that he's very patient with you, and that's a good thing. We approve!"

"What if I don't approve?"

"Let him go. Don't string him along trying to prove he's like Richard. He's not."

She cringed hearing her father refer to the bane of her past by name.

"I mean I don't know. Yes, Xavier is kind, giving, caring and I really have no complaints. And I never do in the beginning. Then they change into who they really are—nothing like who they portrayed!"

"My darling Mira, it is not like you to be indecisive." Her mother's shift from direct to caring unnerved her too.

"Mom, I am not being indecisive. I really do not

know what I want."

"You can't love people afraid of how it will turn out. It's not fair to them, nor is it fair to you."

"What your mother is trying to say is you deserve to be happy, settled and treasured with whomever you choose."

"Yeah well, I was just fine by myself."

"Ha! You were not!"

"Susana, enough. I am tired of cleaning up your language for today. Mira gets to choose. It's her life! All we can offer is our wisdom."

He then turned to her, looking over his glasses to make sure she knew he was talking to her.

"Mira, you figure it out. If you really want to be alone, let this man know, and walk away. If you want to be with him, give your heart. We've taught you how to do that. Go practice!"

With that her father folded his newspaper, and rose from the recliner. "Come my dear, well-meaning wife. Let's leave Mira to sort herself out."

"Yes dear." Her mother pursed her lips, and rose from the sofa.

They both came and kissed her forehead, as she leaned back in her beloved wing back chair—a favorite place to be when summoned home for Sunday dinner. She dare not say anything else when her parents had concluded. She'd learned that lesson as a young girl. Being "lippy" included the longest lectures, and her parents could be extremely persuasive both being lawyers.

As she slouched down, she put her pink toed feet onto the matching ottoman. She really did need to get her act together.

Chapter 34

Later that night…

Mira had left her parents' house, and had found her way to Xavier's place. She was in a good mood. Her parents had been pleasant to Xavier and that was a feat unto itself, especially her mother. They were lounging on his bed comfortably laying across it. The television was on mute. Yes, another soccer match was on. Playing in the background was soft, jazzy music. They both declared when she arrived that they would not multitask—a no work zone for the night.

"What if we got married?" He said as he cuddled her.

"Are you serious? The sex is good and let's not get carried away!" She didn't lift her head or even react. Perhaps her heartbeat sped up.

"I'm not proposing yet. And I don't want to ever keep secrets from you."

"I appreciate that. Secrets, as you have seen, would be a quick way to end this."

"It's not in my nature. I'm straight, if nothing else. So tell me what about us and getting married?"

"I don't think I'm ready to get married. That's a big

step!”

“Why not? We’re compatible. We love each other. Your parents like me. My Papa, Tia, Tio and the family adore you. I haven’t met your grandmother yet, and I’m sure she will like me too!”

“It’s not about you. My parents have a partnership and they love each other. People nowadays don’t want forever. They want until the next best thing comes along.”

“Who said I’m like that?”

“I’m not saying you are. And we are from two totally different worlds.”

“Not so different. My parents were together from their youth until Mama died. Married and committed to each other similar to your parents.”

“You’re missing my point!” She said emphatically, still choosing to not change her position.

“Am I?”

“Yes America and Spain, two countries separated by lots of water.”

“Why have you been by yourself Mira? You know, before me?” He seemed undeterred in asking more questions. She saw no reason not to give her opinions.

"I guess it's easier that way." She said nonchalantly. It was always what she told herself. Nothing risked, nothing lost.

"How can you say that? You're beautiful, full of adventure and you are constantly looking out for others! You're a perfect mate."

"Thank you. All those are 'model' traits in theory."

"I think there's more to it than that. Will you tell me someday?"

"Someday is never coming Xavier. It's an illusion. All we have is now."

"Let me amend my earlier statement. You are also real and very practical!"

She laughed. "Yes, that I am," she said rolling onto her back. She trained her eyes up at the ceiling. Perhaps a moment of solitude, breaking connection to his inquisition. She suspected he was not done. Briefly she closed her eyes, waiting.

"Why not give your love forever?"

She turned her head, looking him in the eye. "Is that what you want?"

"I don't know. I think so."

"See. That's my point!" She dare not turn away.

"I am being straight with you, si? This is unusual for me to be in this position."

"In bed, with a woman?"

"No, not that. I mean you and me," he pointed to her and then back to himself. "I haven't been someone who approaches women. Typically, they find me. I let them chose the rules and they typically never expect anything serious. Perhaps it comes with the reputation of my cousins and their lifestyles. Women who want convenience, a hookup, invites onto the red carpets, to be seen at the right parties." He shrugged.

"Are you saying those women are all shallow?"

"I am not. I am saying I was conveniently available."

"You could have declined their attention."

"Si, I could have. The path of least resistance and the perfect rouse. My cousins rarely suspect I am there to watch over and keep them out of trouble. Or at least that is my intention."

"You have not been one hundred percent successful on that score, according to the tabloids. What is it they call it, '*How could anyone escape the lure of the Gutierrez mystique?*'"

"I can't believe you are still reading that garbage. We're nothing like how they portray us. We might be photographed in those places, and everything else they say is lies! Every single time, their lies inflict havoc and it hurts people."

"There was little else in the public domain about you, a man of international intrigue. No business dealings, no serious romantic entanglements…"

"I do my best to keep it that way, and still sometimes I fail. The work I do is for the good of our family and our businesses. There are times when I'm expected to have a date, a beautiful woman on my arm; other times when they show up mid-event and we are seen together."

"I know nothing about the world you describe."

"You don't have to. It is full of pretense. I've never found myself in a committed, long term relationship. With you, it's different. You are real. I like being in your presence. I want so much to know everything about you, share in your next adventure, take up all your time."

"That's funny!" She half-heartedly chuckled, turning her attention back to the ceiling.

"Why such humor? It is my truth."

"You misunderstand. It's not your truth that I find ironic. I am just like those women. I pursued the men I thought I wanted to be with. I gave them my all. They took every bit of my energy and used it to serve their needs with little or no regards for mine. I taught them what it was like to be loved. And they didn't appreciate nor honor it. I just don't pick right. I finally realized I could thrive by myself."

"That is my good fortune for their stupidity to ever let you go."

"Perhaps those men were stupid. And perhaps I am better off without any of them. My company is profitable and I get to make dreams come true. Damn them!"

"What about your dreams?"

"Trust and believe that I fulfill them every day right along with my clients. That's how I got the idea to start this company. Giving myself permission to have what I want. To be fulfilled."

"Except not in relationship?"

"I didn't say that. Enough of this unproductive talk!" She threw her hands up as if to declare she was done with this discussion.

"Seems as if we are both fishes out of water in our situation, si?" He put his hand over hers.

She continued to look away not wanting to be swayed. It was one of the most intimate moments of her existence. At least it was an intimate moment in which she fully clothed.

"Look at me, Mira!"

She turned back towards him. She could see his determined stare. His eyes mesmerized her like an elixir of a drug. She was entranced and afraid to admit she was becoming addicted.

"I chose you this time, and you didn't pursue me."

"Yes, I guess you're right. And it's not comfortable being this position, this situation."

"Yet it is not unpleasant, si?"

"Si, it is not."

"Well let's just see where it takes us. So far, it has been amazing!" He said holding her hand and pressing it to his lips.

"Okay!" She agreed. "Now, really, can we do something else?"

"Si, I have the perfect idea!"

"What's that?" Mira smiled as if she didn't already know.

"How about you spend the night, and I will make you forget all your worries? You will not have a care in the world."

"Now that is a deal made in heaven!" And those were the last words spoken before he kissed her…

****

The next morning…

"Buenos Dias, querida, officially," he said kissing her again.

"Good Morning Xavier, officially!" Mira said stretching out on the bed, twisted in the sheet. She looked over at the clock and it was half past six. After making love multiple times into the wee hours of the morning, Mira realized the sun was coming up on a new day.

"I've been thinking. You've taught me how to love, to live to be in this moment. I want forever with you Mira. Marry me?"

"Not this again!"

"Si, this…marry me?"

"No."

"No? Not even a consideration? But you love me, si?"

"I do love you. It's easy to love you Xavier." She placed her hand on his cheek.

"So what's the problem with marrying me?"

318

She sat up in the bed, realizing her state of undress as the sheet fell exposing her chest. "It's not you. It's me, my values and home training. When I marry it will be forever!"

He sat up too, turning her face towards his. "Si, that would make me very happy because I never want to let you go."

"You say that right now. And I believe you think that right now. What about tomorrow and the next day?"

"You're not the insecure type, Mira."

"I'm not. And this is your first real relationship. You might change your mind, want a different flavor, a different women. Been there with that one."

"I will not change my mind. Wait, you've been married before? Why didn't you tell me?"

"You didn't ask." She turned away blinking to block out the tears starting to form. Their perfect morning waking up in bed together had now become something else.

"I'm asking now!" She heard him quietly say at her left side. She too preferred that side of the bed and acquiesced to him. She would not acquiesce her hand in marriage.

"Mira, please tell me?"

Without turning or adding any melodrama to her voice, she began.

"Once, a long time ago, my boyfriend of two years and I eloped. It didn't last more than six months. I ended it after I found out he was having an affair with an office worker. All of a sudden, I wasn't the perfect wife for him. I didn't make the right foods, keep the apartment clean enough, wasn't sexy enough. He was coming home late every night, saying he had special projects to work on. I got out, noting our youth and my naïveté. My parents were very supportive."

"Mira, he was a fool! I am not him, nor am I foolish! You are the most precious part of my life. When I am with you, damn everything else. And I know you see I am as giving in our relationship as you are. We are a perfect match!"

She couldn't let his words in. She had to stop this before she fell on her face, yet again. What is that infamous song, *Fools Fall in Love*.

"Look, I am not laying my issues at your feet."

"Come here?"

 She didn't move. He scooped her up and placed her on his lap.

 "I love you, Mira. When you are comfortable with the idea of marrying me, I will be here. Until then, no worries."

She laid her head against his shoulder as he held her in the embrace she needed, and placed her hand on his chest. She felt such warmth with him.

"I have a new idea! Let's live together! I could content myself with that. I desire to come home to you every night, my love. I will prove to you I am not going anywhere. I will not be changing my mind about you, about an us forever and ever."

She lifted her head from the cozy warmth of his body to look into his eyes.

"But, will that be frowned upon in your family?"

"Damn them! I am a man who makes his own choices. I don't want to compete for your love. I choose you on whatever terms you'll have me. Coming home to you every day would make me the luckiest man on the planet!"

All Mira could see was love and devotion from someone who always put her first, considered her needs before his own, and listened to her. "You have a deal Senor Gutiérrez. Let's seal it with a kiss?"

Their lips met and he turned her back onto the bed never breaking their connection. As she was swept up in his all-consuming heat, she let go of her reservations. This compromise suited her needs. Their perfect morning of lovemaking picked up where it left off. For now all his crazy marriage talk was laid to rest, or at least it seemed to be… The next moment and details of "living together" would get sorted at the appointed time. *Celebrate this moment!* And she did let go of all thought to focus on her unbridled passion for this man, Xavier, the love of her life.

Chapter 35

*"If you believe, then you have already taken the first
step towards your achievement."*
~ Rickson Gracie

Jaen, Spain

Buenos Dias Tia!

His aunt looked up from the book she was reading.
The front door was never locked. No one bothered
any of the Gutierrez properties here in Spain, not
wanting the wrath of a protective brood nor the wish
of bad karma in harming such benevolent
benefactors.

"Hola mi sobrino. Come give me a proper greeting!"
It wasn't a request.

"Of course Tia." He walked across the huge expanse
of a room, to stop in front of her as she sat in one of a
pair of wingback, brown leather chairs. He leaned
over and kissed both the cheeks of his favorite aunt.
She loved being in this front room; and most days
this was her perch. That way she could see the
comings and goings of the estate.

"Have a seat." Again not a request.

He took a seat in the chair opposite hers.

"What brings you out this way from the city?"

"I'm looking for Tio Antonio. Is he around?"

"He took a walk down to the stables. Alberto is showing off a new horse."

"A horse? I thought Alberto was into cars, not horses."

"I suppose married life does that."

"I wouldn't know anything about that."

"How's Mira? Is she still putting up with your need to control?"

"Now Tia, where's your faith in my charm?" He smiled.

"Yes I do know you can be charming. And that is beside the point. Real love always wins out. That is unless you screw it up."

"I won't screw it up Tia! Since we're living together, I'm getting lots of practice."

"What do you mean you're living together?"

"Mira and I decided to move in together a couple of weeks ago."

"That's unacceptable!"

"Tia, you have to understand, I can't make her be ready to get married. Mira said she is not ready, and I respect that."

"Why not? You were not raised to milk the cows. You buy the cow before you get to have the milk!"

"I'm not sure Mira would appreciate the animal analogy."

"Xavier, don't be flippant with me! You are not too old for me to beat you with a stick."

"Si Tia. Por favor." He raised his hands in supplication.

"I expect you to make a proper relationship of marriage and then have babies, not shack up like animals who simply want the benefits!"

"I'm aware. I'm working on it. Mira said no to getting married. So I suggested we live together to show her we are well suited and I will not change my mind."

"What did you do to give her pause?"

"It wasn't me. Well at least not exactly. I just have a lot of bad press."

"Oh, you mean you and my son Tomas' wild ways from all those parties?"

"Si. She thinks I'm an international playboy who only wants to be married temporarily until the next best woman comes along."

Tia just shook her head, and set her book aside. Then she rose from the chair and walked away.

He exhaled as he watched his aunt retreat. A longer stern lecture would have been better than seeing disappointment in her eyes.

At the doorway, she turned to look back at him. "Xavier, don't mess this up! Mira is perfect for you. Figure out how to make her your wife, and make some babies!"

He rubbed both his hands over his face. He had left Mira four thousand miles away in Florida, and he hoped eventually she'd give in. He admired her resolve to know for sure, even though he had no doubts he wanted forever with her. Living together was his best alternative right now. Tia would come around, or so he hoped.

****

The Next Day

New York, NY

"Hola Papa!"

"Mi hijo. What are you doing here? What's wrong?" His dad set his paper down on his lap. He was in his favorite chair, a recliner in front of a large screen television that was rarely on.

"I came to visit."

"Si, and it's Thursday. You're never here on Thursday."

"I'm going away for the weekend, so I thought I'd stop through."

"Well next time, call first!"

"Papa, then you'd say don't come."

"Well you don't have to come check on me like I'm some bambino."

"May I sit?"

"Only if you will not lecture me."

"I just want to visit." Xavier raised his hands in helpless defense.

They made small talk for the next fifteen minutes or so. His dad had returned to his perusal of the daily *New York Times* newspaper.

"Mira and I have decided to live together."

"Interesting," his dad said, not looking up from his newspaper.

“I love having her near me.”

“Here?”

“Anywhere! Whether we are in Florida, Spain or traveling for work, I love that she is there.”

“No, mi hijo. Are you going to live here in NY?”

“Sorry Papa. No, we’re going to buy a house at some point in Florida.”

“Oh okay.”

“She’s concerned that I just bought the house for you, and I suggested we pick out a house of our own.”

“Oh okay.”

“Papa! What do you really think of my news?”

He looked up, and Xavier could see his father’s obsidian colored eyes over the rim of his reading glasses. “I learned a long time ago to keep my opinions to myself.”

“Tia sure doesn’t!”

“Yes well Dear Catherine is a very strong woman. Your mother too would have had an opinion.”

“What would Mama have said?” In moments like these, Xavier missed the opportunity to share with his mother, wondering what her advice might be. He was convinced she would have loved Mira.

"She'd say, don't waste your life away waiting for the perfect time. It never comes and you might regret waiting."

"That sort of sounds like Tia."

"I believe Gutiérrez men have that in common–-marrying strong-willed women who boss us around!"

"Oh Papa, I'm sure you were no pushover, and gave as good as you got!"

"I miss your Mama. She always knew the right thing to say and do."

"I miss her too!"

"She'd be happy for you, even if you are shacking up to steal the milk without buying the cow."

"Papa, really? You and Tia have conspired against me!"

Xavier watched his father laugh. It was a rare thing as his dad mostly grumbled, and complained about his arthritis. This was a good moment, even though it was awkward talking about Mira and his decision to live together, instead of marry.

"I'm not your Tia. So I say go and enjoy your life on whatever terms you want. It's yours to live. I've always been proud of you and Matias. You deserve to be happy!"

"Thanks Papa." He went over and hugged his father. Relishing that he still had his Papa alive and to whom he could ask advice.

"Yeah, yeah, yeah. I have dominoes soon in the community room. Wanna come?"

"No thanks. That's my cue to go. I have a flight to catch to get home to Mira. We hope you'll come back to Florida soon. Love you Papa!" Xavier picked up his jacket, lovingly slapped his father's back and let himself out.

Epilogue

"Will you give me yourself? Will you come travel with me? Shall we stick by each other as long as we live? ~ Walt Whitman

Later that night – Ponte Vedra, FL

Xavier let himself into the house that Mira had helped him select for his Papa. As soon as he closed the door, he could smell food. Had Mira cooked? He loosened his tie, and pulled off his jacket.

"Hola Mira, Mira," he said walking into the kitchen. He paused at the counter as her back was to him. He liked the view of her backside bending over.

"You're back just in time for dinner!" She said, pulling a dish from the oven. He watched her set the covered dish on the trivet, and remove the hot mitts. He kissed her briefly on the lips.

"You're cooking?"

"More like warming up. Tia Catherine sent her lasagna."

"What do you mean she sent her lasagna?"

"I know. It's kind of crazy! It arrived via airmail as a surprise. It included a set of instructions for our dinner, and a sealed note we were supposed to read together after dinner. You know I'm not much of a cook. So we were going to have a salad. I've set the table, and was just waiting for you to warm the bread."

"Wait, my aunt sent food from España?"

"Yes. That is correct."

"She's too much!"

"She made us her famous lasagna. That's her way of saying she forgives us for living together."

"I don't understand."

"Tia believes in marriage. When I told her we were living together, she was not happy with me and walked out. Actually, I think she was disappointed. In delivering the lasagna, she is sending an olive branch to me. To us!"

"Oh, that's brilliant. She also sent a bottle of extra virgin olive oil—your family's brand. The instructions said 'just in case we didn't have any in our new home.'" Mira held up the bottle.

Xavier just closed his eyes, and took a deep breath. "Tia thinks ahead."

"When I got home from the store, I had already brought salad, wine, cheese and bread. She must have known."

"She is very wise, and somewhat meddlesome. It's a little scary that she can foresee our desires being fulfilled."

"Well this Spanish lasagna smells amazing!"

Xavier laughed. "It's actually an Italian lasagna that Tia Catherine has made her own. It's excelente!"

Mira looked confused.

"I'll tell you more while we're eating. How can I help with dinner? And by the way, I like this domestic side of you."

"Oh please! You are going to learn to cook right along with me. Now, go get washed up. Dinner will be ready in fifteen minutes."

"Si Senorita!" Xavier said as he popped a carrot stick in his mouth from the salad bowl, and tapped her on the backside.

"I'm gonna get you for that!"

"Oh please punish me," he said jokingly as he spun around to walk out of the kitchen.

As promised, fifteen minutes later they were seated out on the deck, just in time for sunset. Mira had lit a couple candles, and Xavier poured the red wine. Each of them had a hunk of lasagna on their plates, a side bowl of salad, communal bread and olive oil for dressing.

She took a bite of the lasagna. Xavier waited for what he knew would come next. Bliss!

"Oh wow, this is amazing!" She said licking her lips after swallowing. She then took another bite and he watched her chew. She was so sexy. She then licked the sauce off the fork.

"Mira, you are making love to that fork, and it is distracting as hell!"

"Oh sorry. Why are you watching me and not eating?"

"It is so much better watching you have Tia's lasagna for the first time."

"Suit yourself. I suppose if you're not going to eat, you could tell me the history of this lasagna?"

He picked up the wine and took a gulp. He definitely needed to focus on something else other than watching her eat.

"An Italian family came to live with the family as caretakers. Francesca, the cook, and Luca, the landscaper. Remember the *Spring Fling*? My cousin TM came in with Lea?"

Mira nodded.

"That's Francesca and Luca's daughter, Rosa Lea. We grew up with her, and her brother,

Luciano. Francesca and Luca were besties with Tia and Tio. We are all familia. So that is how the recipe became a family tradition."

"Your family is fascinating!" Mira said sipping on her wine now that her plate was empty.

"All families have their stories. Just like you and I are crafting a story of our own."

"Hmmm, I suppose you're right. Cheers to good times," he watched her lift the glass with a smile. He raised his glass to hers.

"Where's Tia's note?"

"Let's finish eating, clear the table and then read it together," Mira said, rising up to carry some of the dishes back into the villa. After he gobbled down Tia's best dish, he helped her carry the rest of the dinnerware inside and load the dishwasher. When the table was cleared, she carried the envelope back with her outside. Xavier had poured them fresh glasses of wine.

"Please open and read what my dear aunt says?"

Mira broke the seal on the white envelope that simply said: Xavier & Mira. He watched as she pulled out a watercolor painted card of a vineyard of olive trees.

> *"Please accept my first housewarming gift of*
> *what I hope will become one of many for the*
> *happy couple! I am elated for you, my nephew*

"That was a nice note. I like them, your family."

"I believe the feeling is mutual ~ the Mira effect! We will have to send a thank you card for Tia's thoughtfulness. But not tonight."

"I got you chocolate ice cream for dessert, my love."

"We should have it inside…in bed?"

"Perhaps," she smiled.

Xavier watched Mira in the moonlight, as the candle blew with the wind. That same wind lifted her curly hair on soft gusts from the ocean breezes. She looked like an angel.

"You have always made me breathless, Mira."

"And you have been trying to charm me since we met."

"I am a man who could care less about charming anyone but you. All I desire is to be with you forever, mi amor."

"Let's go have dessert, as you suggested, mi amor. In bed…"

The End and To Be Continued…

Will Mira give in to Xavier's desire to marry? Will she finally commit to forever?

About the Author:

L. Elaine lives in Maryland, just outside her hometown of Washington, DC. She has three sons, a daughter-in-law, a granddaughter and grandson—both whose eyes sparkle each time they get a new idea! Priceless to watch…

Almost a decade ago. with coaxing from a dear friend at work, she decided to write her own romance novel to see if she would enjoy crafting beautiful stories of love set in exotic locales. And she does, so she continues to write.

Besides reading and writing, L. Elaine enjoys traveling, teaching, meeting people and tasting food from foreign lands. She considers herself a lifelong learner with lots left to discover! She would love to hear from you so please visit her website.

<u>EXCERPT</u>

from the next book

in the series

Dynasty of Love

The Gutiérrez Family: Book 6

And stay tuned for more love stories from the *Dynasty of Love* series about the Gutiérrez family!

Tomas Miguel and Rosa Lea's Story…excerpt:

Tomas Miguel let the phone ring. One, two, three...*where is she*? Four, five...he was about to hang up, when he heard her answer.

"I'll reiterate to you, I have never been good at long distance relationships." Rosa Lea sighed as she leaned back in her chaise lounge chair staring down at the stack of tabloid magazines that held stories of him at his latest partying fiasco.

"Yes, I know," he said as he laid back across the bed in his quiet hotel suite. He held the phone in his left hand and rubbed his eyes with his right. "I miss you Lea, seeing you smile, holding you in my arms. The memory of your sweet kisses isn't enough. I want you here with me now." He paused, his mind racing. "Why don't you get on a plane and come spend a few days with me here in Paris."

She ignored his request, still dealing with how intense her feelings for him run. "I just saw you a few days ago. Yet it seems like it could've been weeks ago. I guess I think of you all the time. I never been much for suppressing my love."

"You are experiencing a lot of lust with some love mixed in. I know the feeling."

"You might be right. Either way I don't like it. This

thing between us is out of control."

"Ha! You think I like being away from you? Especially now? This trip could not be helped. Business is crazy right now. I have another week here before I can return to Spain."

"Seeing you partying the night away doesn't look like you are working hard at business!" She lifted a tabloid magazine, read the caption and dropped it back on the table. "These pictures show you smiling, dancing, celebrating…"

"You're jealous. I like that, even though your concerns are unfounded. I was out with clients. They insisted on showing me a good time. It would be rude not to go, not to enjoy their hospitality. Trust me, looking at or hooking up with any other woman doesn't interest me. I have you! What do I need them for? Plus, it's not my style."

"Really? I read all about your reputation as the international playboy businessman. Plenty of women are willing to keep you company while you are away!"

"I don't want them. I don't want anyone but you, querida. Lea, you are a big part of my heart. I want you and I get what I want."

"What happens when you get tired of me?"

"It's not happening now, so why talk about it?" He was careful not to be glib or feed into her misconceptions. Best to stick with reality. Plus, he was tired and called to hear her voice before he went to bed. It would not take her place, and it was the perfect melody to calm him. He loved talking to Lea. She let him talk about anything he wanted, and she was very smart, intuitive, and could often read his next thought before he spoke it. She was special.

"I don't know. I'm all confused. See why it's not working?"

He chuckled. "Oh, we work! We make each other happy. We are very good together like a spicy dish. We have passion and chemistry. You are saucy and I love your company. I will be home soon and we will continue where we left off. My offer stands for you to come to Paris. In the meantime, I wanted to ring and wish you sweet dreams."

"Thanks for saying all that!" She smiled. "I'll think about coming to Paris. I miss you too. Sweet dreams back to you and good night!"

She hung up the phone, picked up all the magazines she had collected with his photos, and dumped them in the trash. She trusted what he said. She had known him all their lives—they grew up together running the hills covered with olive groves. He'd been like a brother to her, until he was not anymore. Their attraction had bloomed into something else. *Time for bed Lea*, she said to herself aloud. She sighed knowing she had multiple classes to teach tomorrow at university. She walked across the room, turned off the lamp and then climbed into her bed. She knew he would consume her dreams as he had done every night since they reconnected.